CAROLINE TRENCH

Nurse to the Island

Originally published as Harlequin Romance #467

Harlequin Books

TORONTO • LONDON • NEW YORK • AMSTERDAM • SYDNEY • WINNIPEG

Original hardcover edition published by Mills & Boon Limited

ISBN 0-373-00467-2

Harlequin edition published June 1959
Reprinted 1959
1960
1971

This Harlequin's Collection edition printed 1976

A special note of interest to the reader

Harlequin Books were first published in 1949. The original book was entitled *The Manatee* and identified as Book No. 1 — since then some two thousand titles have been published.

As readers are introduced to Harlequin Romances, very often they wish to obtain older titles. To supply this demand, Harlequin prints an assortment of "old" titles every year. Some are made available to all bookselling stores via special Harlequin Jamboree displays. Others are appearing in the Harlequin's Collection series.

As these books are exact reprints of the original Harlequin Romances, you may indeed find a few typographical errors, etc., because we apparently were not as careful in our younger days as we are now. Nonetheless, we hope you enjoy this "old" reprint and apologize for any errors you may find.

Printed in Canada

CHAPTER ONE

JAN LEANED OVER the side of the ship, watching the three figures disappear among the crowds, and she blinked her eyes fiercely. It was her own fault, of course; she had asked them not to stay any longer. Soon the bell telling visitors to disembark would ring, and she had had a horrible feeling that if her father and mother and Roderick were with her then, she would give way and burst into tears.

That, of course, would be absurd — more than absurd. She set her lips very tightly and concentrated upon her luck in getting this job in the West Indian island, so small that no ordinary maps even marked it. She had just passed her S.R.N. examination and was working in a busy London hospital when she developed pneumonia. It happened on the day she got engaged to Roderick and life was wonderful; she was even more than usually busy in hospital and she was going to meet Roderick's people. So, at first, she had refused to give in, with the result that when she collapsed she was much worse than she would otherwise have been, and the doctor not only advised a winter abroad but found the job on Dream Island for her. A job after her own heart.

If only—she gazed after the place where her parents and Roderick had disappeared, as though looking could bring them back to her—if only she did not have to leave Roderick! One tiny part of her heart said, "If he loved you as much as you love him, he would have walked off with you, married you straight away and taken you abroad for a honeymoon." But she pushed this thought away so quickly that it was scarcely there at all. Roderick was a young, ambitious barrister who had a future, so everyone said. But the "future" had not yet arrived and he couldn't afford to marry yet; she would not have let him, if it came to that. If only his mother, when Jan had stayed at Roderick's home, had not shown so plainly that she thought that Jan was not good enough for him, that he needed someone with influence or money; if only she had not exaggerated Jan's bout of pneumonia into a weak lung that would leave her a semi-invalid! But Roderick knew that that was not true; Roderick had a mind of his own and he loved her. He would go on loving her, however long they were parted. And, after all, Jan only expected to be away for a few months—a year at the longest. Nevertheless, she shivered without realizing that she was doing so.

"Are you cold?" a voice at her side asked. "The wind has turned very chilly now."

She looked round quickly. Dr. Nicolas Duncarron, her employer-to-be, was standing by her side. He looked as though he really minded whether she were cold or not, and looking at his tall, broad figure, the strong, far-from-handsome face with dark hair and deep grey eyes, she told herself again how lucky she was to have a man like this to work under.

"No, not exactly cold," she answered him. "Just a goose walking over my grave."

"It's saying good-bye, isn't it?" he asked in a tone that made her realize that he understood. "I always feel exactly the same, even though my home's in Dream Island now. You'll feel better by tomorrow and all ready to enjoy the rest of the voyage. A new experience—it is new, isn't it? And, I hope, a very pleasant one."

He leant companionably over the rail by her side and went on. "Do you mind if I stay and talk for a while? Leslie's saying good-bye to Griselda and they don't want me there. Les and I will be flying out tomorrow, so we'll be there, ready to greet you when you reach Dream Island, but Griselda's nervous about travelling by air, and the sea trip ought to do you good."

She nodded without answering. There seemed no need of speech somehow with this big man with the ugly, understanding face. He gave you an impression of standing solidly by you without words being spoken. He knew about Roderick and about her feelings at leaving him and, without saying anything, he was telling her that he understood. She felt better already and wished that he was travelling with them.

He went on, "Leslie and I went out to Dream Island when an uncle of ours left us the fruit estate there. I act as his partner on the estate, as I expect you know, and I look after all the people on it, too. But it has always been my dream to open a hospital there. Any seriously ill cases have to go to Jamaica, and at times the delay and the long journey can be very serious for them. But fruit estates don't pay as well as all that, and any profits we do make have to go back into the land. So it looked as though it would never come true."

"But it has," she reminded him.

"Yes, it has," he agreed with a smile that lit up his face and made little laughter-wrinkles at the sides of his eyes. "Another uncle died and left me some money, so I'm using every penny of it to get my hospital started. For goodness' sake, don't expect anything elaborate. It'll seem horribly primitive to you, and at present I've only got a wooden hut for the building, though I hope to improve on that later. But you'll find yourself district nurse as well as hospital nurse, so I hope you're not absolutely daunted by the idea of the work. I'll try not to be too hard a taskmaster, but I'm inclined to forget how hard I'm driving people when I get on my pet hobby-horse."

"I'm looking forward to it," she assured him. "I enjoy work."

"Good! I hope you won't regret those words before you've finished with me!" But his smile faded away, to be replaced by a serious, worried expression as he went on, "But nursing is one thing and acting as companion to a neurotic woman is another, and, between you and me, I'm afraid that my sister-in-law, Griselda, is as neurotic as they make them. Leslie has been terribly worried. He sees the difference in her from the gay, happy girl he married, and he thinks there must be something physically wrong with her. As you're living with us, he's hoping that you'll do her good. And I dare say the very fact of having another girl to talk to will help her a lot by chasing away her loneliness and giving her an interest in life. That's what she needs if their marriage isn't to go on the rocks entirely. But it's not going to be easy for you, and it's putting a lot on your shoulders on top of your real work. I'm talking so plainly because I feel that if you object, it would be better to find another house where you can lodge."

His eyes, looking down at her, were very serious now. They seemed to bore right into her mind and read her thoughts. She had met Griselda, Dr. Duncarron's brother's wife, and she knew that she would not be an easy person to live with. She appreciated Nicolas' candour, especially as she knew he had not found it easy to talk so openly. She knew, equally, that she could neither let him down nor refuse to help an unhappy woman who was desperately lonely and out of place on a small island with little social life. So she met his eyes frankly and smiled as she said, "I know all that. But I like what I've seen of Mrs. Duncarron and if I can help her at all by being there, I'll be only too glad."

He gave a long sigh of relief, which showed how anxiously he had been waiting for her answer. Then, as the bell for visitors to go ashore rang through the ship, he held out his hand. "Au revoir, then, and thank you," he said. "Have a good voyage. We'll come and meet you both at Jamaica and go on to Dream Island with you."

Leslie Duncarron came up to them before Jan could reply.

"Ready, Nick?" he asked. "Well, it's good-bye for a short time, Miss Lorrimer. *Bon voyage!*—and look after Griselda for me, won't you?"

His sunburnt face looked strained and anxious as he said the last words. He was a couple of years younger than Nicolas, a couple of inches shorter, his hair fairer, his eyes less dark. But he looked so worried as he spoke that Jan assured him that she would make quite sure that Mrs. Duncarron was as fit as could be by the time they reached Kingston.

"But enjoy yourself, too," Nicolas reminder her. "Remember, this is a holiday for you. Your work starts when you reach Dream Island."

But Leslie was fidgeting now to be gone.

"Come on, Nick," he repeated, and started to make his way towards the gangway.

Jan hurried down to her cabin. Nicolas had cheered her up, but even so she felt she could not bear the feeling of irrevocability that watching the raising of the gangway and the slow widening of the passage between ship and shore would give her. She unpacked with fierce intensity, stowing everything away neatly in the small space provided, trying to choke back her recurring homesickness and her longing for Roderick and her thoughts of them all bundling into Dr. Lorrimer's car, turning its bonnet towards the dear familiarity of home.

She squeezed her eyes tightly, for when she did that, Roderick's face danced before her, the almost golden wave of his hair, deep-blue eyes whose color seemed to intensify or pale with every mood. Then she opened them quickly again, because she must not think of the increasing miles that separated them. She looked instead at her own face in the mirror, the short, clustering curls of chestnut-brown, the eyes that seemed to take their color from her mood, so that no one quite knew whether they were brown, amber, green or grey, and turned away with a sigh. There was no denying it, she told herself; she was a very ordinary sort of wife for a man like Roderick to choose.

She moved back impatiently to her unpacking, trying to think of the new scenes, the beauty and excitement, the interest of the work before her. Her loneliness would pass, she knew, but it was hard to ignore it while it lasted.

When she had finished, she went along to Griselda Duncarron's stateroom to see if there was anything she could do to help. Its limited space seemed to be completely covered. To begin with, there were so many flowers that there appeared to be little room for anything else. Suitcases and cabin trunks, half unpacked, littered the floor, while Griselda sat in the one easy-chair, her lovely red hair loosened round her thin face, sharp lines of weariness etched into her cheeks.

Her face lit up, however, when she saw Jan.

"Oh, nurse, I'm so glad you've come!" she cried. "I'm absolutely at my wits' end! I'm the worlds worst sailor, to begin with, and with no sense of tidiness at all. I got as far as this with my unpacking and now I'm feeling too rotten to go on, so I'm simply in despair!"

"Why don't you lie down on your bunk while I unpack for you?" Jan suggested—a suggestion which Griselda obeyed so quickly that Jan, deciding she had been waiting for it, gave an inward grin as she wondered what would have happened if her help had not been offered.

"I hope we're going to get on," Griselda continued, watching her as she went deftly about the work of putting everything into place. "We're sure to be on top of each other all the time. As a matter of fact, I think we shall. I take immediate likes and dislikes to people and I really do think that since Nick insists upon having someone for his precious new place, you're the best choice he could have made. I don't know whether you'll be able to put up with me, though. I get bored stiff and then I make everyone suffer."

"I daresay I shall bear it," Jan told her, rather dryly, and Griselda laughed.

"Oh, I know I deserve shaking, and it's a great pity Leslie doesn't do it every once in a while," she answered. "But you've no idea what it's like. Absolutely deadly dull. The same faces day after day and not a thing to do. No dances because there aren't enough of us, no theatre or pictures, of course; only the radio besides any amusements we can make for ourselves. I'm a crowd-loving sort of person; I like lots of noise and people, and I like having friends to drop in at any time of day and going out to dinner and parties and making everyone jealous when I wear new dresses. So I get fed up and just nag and lead Leslie the hell of a life. I'm warning you."

She was so open about it all that Jan could do nothing but laugh. However, she remembered Leslie's anxiety and asked seriously, "Isn't there anything you could get really interested in out there?"

Griselda sat up on her bunk, hugging her knees. She looked little more than a child at that moment, and certainly a most fascinating, if infuriating, one. She shrugged her shoulders in answer to Jan's inquiry.

"Oh, if I wanted to be earnest and serious-minded and go in for good works and be interested in the workers on the estate, I expect there's a lot," she answered frankly. "But I'm one of the lilies that toil not, you know. Work doesn't appeal to me in the least. It's social life I want. And there are only two other estates on the island. One belongs to an American, Joe Anderson, who isn't interested in anything but his work. He hasn't got a wife—she's divorced or dead; I never found out which—and Sarah-Ann, his daughter, has only just left school and come to the island. Luis Corando, who owns the other estate, is interesting, but he has a deadly stick of a manager and isn't often there himself. He has too many business interests elsewhere —made his money in oil or something, and he's more of a business man than a farmer. He and Leslie don't get on, anyway, because he wants to buy up Golden Grove and has been rather persistent about it since Nick and Leslie first refused. Though why that should affect me, I don't know. Still—there you are!"

Jan would have liked to have gone on listening to tales of the inmates of the island that was to be her home, but her trained eye noticed how white and ill Griselda was looking, and she asked, "Wouldn't you like to get to bed? I've got all your things cleared up now, so I can brush your hair and help you get undressed if so."

"Jan, you're an angel!" Griselda declared, as she moved to sit at the dressing-table. "I'm going to call you Jan. We're all on Christian-name terms on the island, so you'd better call me Griselda. I do hate leaving England, only if I stayed, I couldn't have Leslie. Why can't I have them both? If only he would sell to Luis—only neither he nor Nick would hear of it. They don't realize——"

She broke off, her small, even, white teeth coming together with a snap. Jan started to brush her wavy, beautiful red hair and she went on, almost fiercely, "Don't you ever marry, Jan! It's absolute torture! Books make it sound as though it's the end of the story, but it isn't; it's only the beginning. You have to fight to keep love; you start out all starry-eyed, thinking everything's going to be like a fairy-story, and you find yourself up against all sorts of little things that work you nearly into a frenzy. Little things are the worst, because if there's still love underneath, big things can usually be forgiven and forgotten, but the little things go on irritating till they become big and love almost gets lost beneath them. You have to be ready to give and take and adapt yourself, and I can't do it. I want to go on having the things I like and having lots of people round me, all spoiling and admiring me. And when nothing at all is what I'd expected, it's too terrible for words. I need admiration as much as I need air, and if I don't get it, I'm bored stiff and I want everyone to know it. I'm a beast to Leslie, I know, but I can't change, so it's time he understood my point of view."

She whirled round on her chair, looking at Jan with wide green eyes, for all the world like a defiant child. Then, suddenly, her expression changed and she broke out laughing.

"Don't take my advice," she said lightly. "Of course, you'll marry your nice barrister man and be absolutely respectable and dutiful and put his career first and never know what it is to be in the seventh heaven or in the depths of hell!"

Jan did not answer. She did not think she quite liked that description of her probable married life. It made her sound smug and unfeeling, and she did not think that the wild, tumultuous beating of her heart whenever she thought of Roderick could be called either.

But it was no use being annoyed with Griselda. She tucked her into her bunk and was just about to leave the cabin when Griselda put out one hand towards her and said in a repentant tone, "Please don't be furious with me when I make your life a misery. I've loads of good intentions now, but they wear off. But I'm glad you're coming and I do want you to stay."

"Oh, I expect I can hold my own," Jan assured her, and went up on deck.

Here, a cold wind was blowing. She pulled her coat collar tightly round her neck and started to walk briskly round. The shore was a tiny black smudge in the grey dreariness of twilight. One star had come out and dark clouds were chasing busily round it as though playing a game to see how near they could come without actually covering it. Jan shivered. The ship seemed suddenly isolated. There was so much sea and soon there would be more of it—limitless sea on all sides with only the smallness of their ship in the midst of it all. It made her feel alone and friendless and very unimportant in the scheme of life.

A voice behind her made her jump.

"It's very lonely, isn't it?" the man who had come up to her asked. "All this—all the immensity." He waved his hand round the darkening scene as she turned quickly. It was strange that he should not only have felt her thoughts, but also put them into words for her.

He was a tall man, slim and very elegant, with a particularity of dress that gave him an un-English air. His voice, too, held a trace of a foreign accent. His hair was black with just a tinge of grey at the temples, and his eyes, keen and direct, were a very dark brown that was almost black.

"I'm sorry; did I startle you?" he asked. "But this is only a small ship and we make friends without formality. You are Miss Janet Lorrimer, I believe, and you are travelling with Mrs. Duncarron?"

"Yes," she agreed. "But how did you know?"

He threw back his head to laugh.

"I should like to pretend that I knew it by magic," he told her. "But I have to admit that I am well in the know here. I travel often by this line and all the officers and stewards know me. I saw you talking to Nicolas Duncarron and I said, 'That girl is like a goddess,' and my steward told me the rest."

She colored a little at the compliment, but, though she certainly did not take it seriously, she had to admit that it pleased her. He went on happily, "We are going to be good friends. It is ordained so, for, of all the tiny islands in the Caribbean, we are both going to the same. I live on Dream Island too."

"You do?" she asked with interest. "How strange! It's only a tiny place, isn't it?"

"That was why I said it was ordained by fate." His voice became formal and he bowed ceremoniously. "Luis Corando, at your service, Senorita," he said.

Thus Jan met the man who was to play so big a part in her future, unaware, at that moment, of the changes that would be brought about in her life through his agency.

CHAPTER TWO

A STORM BLEW UP during the night, and the next day mountainous seas, a strong wind and a spatter of rain made things very disagreeable on deck. Jan would have enjoyed battling against the storm, nevertheless, but Griselda showed that she was making no idle complaint when she had told Jan that she was a bad sailor. She was also an extremely depressed and gloomy one, and Jan felt it only fair that she should spend a good deal of her time in trying to cheer her up and doing all she could to ease the sickness. So she herself was able to spend very little time on deck. She met most of the passengers without having much chance to make friends amongst them, but Luis Corando sought her out each time she emerged from Griselda's cabin and marched her firmly round the deck or played deck games with her.

"You will lose that pretty color if you do not get this fresh air," he told her. "You are young, and a sea journey should be a time of pleasure and amusement for you; you should not be thinking all the time of other people. I am only sorry that I am not young and handsome so that we could have the shipboard romance, eh? But I am afraid that I am not the maiden's young dream. You say that, yes?"

"Yes. I mean——" Jan found herself becoming involved. "You're not old, but I don't want a shipboard romance. That's not what I came for at all."

"No?" He raised his eyebrows at her. "Then there is a young man at home, I take it?"

"There is," she acknowledged. "But it doesn't follow. Even if I was completely unattached I might not want a—a shipboard romance."

"Oh, no!" He laughed disbelievingly. "You can never make me believe that! I know too much about women and their ways, I assure you, and in my experience they are always willing to flirt, given a warm moonlight night and a silver sea around. And the right man, of course."

Yes, she expected he did, indeed, know quite a lot about women. Too much for their peace of mind, perhaps. Not that it would affect her; even if her whole heart and mind had not been taken up by Roderick, he was not the sort of man she would ever fall in love with, though she might—and did—enjoy his company. Love, thought Jan, meant trust, and somehow she did not think she would ever altogether trust Luis Corando.

"Are you married?" her train of thought carried her on to ask.

"What—me?" His mobile eyebrows shot up again in mock horror. "Indeed, no, and I do not suppose I ever shall be. Just think of the boredom of being tied to one woman all my life! I like to move from one to another."

"Well, as long as they all know that——" Jan was beginning dryly, when the luncheon gong boomed through the ship and she left him to get ready for the meal.

The next day was calmer and already much warmer. Jan, feeling the soft touch of a refreshing breeze on her cheek, went down to persuade Griselda to come on deck.

"You'll never feel better as long as you stuff down here," she said frankly. "And I shan't go on waiting on you if you don't make an effort."

Griselda pulled a face.

"You're a bully, Jan!" she declared. "And I'm looking absolutely hideous! I simply couldn't bear to be seen looking like this. First impressions make all the difference."

"You'll look fine when I've finished with you," Jan promised her. "And you know some of the people on board. You've met Luis Corando, haven't you?"

"Luis Corando?" A gleam of interest lit up Griselda's eyes. "Why didn't you tell me he was on board?"

"I didn't think of it," Jan confessed. "And you said you didn't like him, so I didn't suppose you'd be particularly interested."

"I said that Leslie and Nicolas didn't like him, which is quite a different thing," Griselda informed her. "All right, Jan. I'll go on deck, but I still feel like a bit of chewed string and I'm sure I look like one."

"Don't fish for compliments," Jan told her calmly. "Let me help you get dressed and I'll do your hair for you."

When, half a hour later, Griselda was ensconced in a chair on deck, a rug wrapped round her and a couple of novels, a packet of cigarettes and a box of chocolates by her side, she looked very far from a piece of chewed string. She was wearing a green suit that brought out all the glints in her cat-like eyes; she looked finished and smart and self-assured, with her careful make-up hiding the pallor of her cheeks and Jan's hair-do showing off the shape of her small, proud head.

Luis strolled along the deck towards them as soon as they were settled and bowed over Griselda's hand.

"I am so glad to see you up and about again Mrs. Duncarron," he said. "I have been most anxious about your health. Jan has kept me informed about it, but she tells me that you were ill in England, too."

Griselda sat up, all the color and sparkle returning to her face.

"Oh, I'm better now," she answered. "Feeling horribly bored at the thought of going back to Dream Island though."

"Bored?" He raised his eyebrows. "But, indeed, that will not do. I hope to spend all winter there and we shall have to do something about keeping you amused. I am thinking of buying a yacht and we shall be able to get up some pleasant trips, I hope. I shall probably have friends to stay with me for a good deal of the time, too. No, you will not be bored, I promise you. How could anyone allow so lovely a lady to be unhappy?"

Griselda preened herself and Jan felt vaguely uneasy. There was really no need for it, she told herself; Griselda had far more experience of the world than Jan herself, and she must have sense enough to see that he did not mean a word he said—that he made the same remarks to every pretty woman he met.

She had no more time, at the moment, to think it over, for a group of young people called to her to join them at deck tennis and she left Griselda and Luis to their own company.

During the next few days she grew to know the other young people much better and, in joining in their amusements, she naturally saw less of Griselda, who did not care for sports. Griselda, in fact, made it abundantly clear that she did not want Jan hanging around her, and it was this fact that worried the girl. She told herself that Griselda was in love with her husband, that she was decent and honourable in spite of her neurotic tendencies, and that she would never allow herself to become serious about another man. But she knew how the desire to be in the limelight, together with boredom with home life, could work slowly but surely to make for an unstable recklessness. And the fact remained that wherever Luis was to be found, there also would be Griselda, that she seemed incapable of talking to, even noticing, anyone else, that her eyes shone when Luis was near and her voice took on a note of excitement, while, when he was away, she became dull and lifeless.

Whatever, wondered Jan, could she do? She remembered Nicolas' words about saving the marriage as though it had already gone very near the rocks, she thought of Leslie's worried face and the anxiety in his voice. There was no real harm in Griselda; Jan could not help liking her. And she simply could not stand by and watch her make a mess both of her own life and her husband's. But what could Jan do about it?

There were only a few more days left of the journey to Jamaica when the answer came. She was standing alone at the rails one evening, watching the flow of the sea and the silver gleam touching the distant horizon, when Luis came up to her and, putting his elbows on the rails, joined her in her peaceful occupation.

"Why haven't I seen anything of you lately?" he asked at last.

She turned to face him squarely.

"I hadn't noticed any particular desire on your part to try and see me," she answered flatly.

He took out his cigarette case and offered her one before replying.

"In most other women I should detect a touch of jealousy in that remark," he said thoughtfully. "But not you—you are not the jealous type, I should say, and in any case I can't flatter myself that you are interested enough in me to mind. No; those were words of disapproval. What have I done to make you look like that?"

"You know quite well," Jan answered. "Tell me straight out that it isn't my business, if you like. But Griselda has been ill; she's in a sort of disturbed state and not quite as well able to judge people as I am. And you may say things you don't mean — turn her head——"

She broke off, coloring. What right had she to act as their mentor? They were both older than she and had every right to resent her interference. But Leslie and Nicolas—— She stood still, feeling uncomfortable and unhappy.

But he only laughed, bending his handsome head close to hers.

"I know; I'm a despicable character," he answered. "I only wish I had as loyal a friend as you are to Griselda, though." Then, suddenly, he dropped his voice to a confidential note. "The trouble is," he said, "that I just have to find someone amusing and not too repulsively ugly to pass the time with on board ship. I suffer boredom no more kindly than I suffer fools. And, as the only two people on board I could bear to be with are you and Griselda, and as you've completely deserted me lately—well, what else is there for me to do? I can assure you, I have no interest at all in the lady, except as a charming companion."

But it wasn't much use telling Griselda that, thought Jan glumly; she wouldn't believe it. But as she was pondering on this fact, he went on slowly, "Now, if you were to take her place, I might consider seeing less of her. In fact, I would gladly do so."

Jan whirled round, her eyes blazing.

"Whatever do you mean?" she demanded. "That's almost like blackmail."

He put his hand on her arm to stop her.

"Yes, I was right," he remarked dispassionately. "You look extremely pretty when you are angry. It makes some girls lovely and others cruelly plain. But I apologize; I should not have teased you. Indeed, there's no blackmail in it, my child. I know your opinion of me and I know you have a lucky young man in England. It would be useless to try to get you to flirt with me. But, strangely enough, I like you quite simply as a friend. And, much as you disapprove of me, I don't think you dislike me. And the more I saw of you, the less I would be alone with the dangerous

Griselda and the less I would be tempted. For she is both dangerous and tempting, you must admit."

Jan was still flushed and uncomfortable, not knowing how far he was amusing himself by teasing her and how much he meant seriously. She had never before met a rich business magnate used to getting his own way in everything—and a handsome, fairly young one with Latin blood in his veins at that—so she had no yardstick by which to measure him. But even though she did not trust him altogether, she found him interesting to be with and there was really no reason why she should cut herself off from his company, just because he had made fun of the whole affair. That was all it was—not the scheming she had at first felt it to be.

So she said reflectively, "You make everything sound so much more than it really is, and I'm no match for you at playing with words. Of course, I enjoy being with you—you know that perfectly well—and if you ask me, I'm quite willing to play games and dance and walk round the deck with you. But don't make it sound underhand, because I don't like that."

He laughed.

"I wouldn't dare suggest anything of the sort to you," he told her with mock terror. "Come on, then; let's start by having a swim."

Griselda came to the swimming-pool to watch them, but she could not swim and did not like going into the water, so she watched Jan's perfect strokes and dives with a sulky expression. She sulked still more when she found her tête-à-têtes with Luis becoming more and more often a threesome. At first she hinted openly to Jan that her presence was not required, but Luis made matters worse by staring at Griselda with a look of surprised innocence.

"Oh, but don't you think that three good friends are more entertaining than two?" he asked blandly. "It's only in love that two's company and three's none, isn't it?"

Griselda got up and flounced away to gloom in her cabin. Jan felt sorry for her; she wanted to run after her and try to straighten things out, but she sensed that putting the situation into words would only make matters worse.

However, there was an unpleasant scene in Griselda's cabin that evening when Jan looked in to see if she could help.

"Help?" Griselda's voice grew shrill. "Nice help you've given me, I must say! Taking Luis away from me!"

"But we're only friends, all three of us," Jan protested. She longed to leave Luis completely alone to prevent any more unpleasantness, but Griselda, sitting there with her eyes huge and sulky and her lips turned downwards, looked little more than a spoilt child. If only she could help to keep her marriage straight till Leslie could meet her and take over! Jan felt illogically so much older than Griselda that she knew she had to do whatever she could to look after her.

"Friends?" Griselda's voice rose shrilly. "Luis Corando doesn't go in for women friends! You're not such a fool as to think he does."

"I'm engaged and you're married," Jan reminded her, quietly. "Luis knows there can be nothing but friendship with either of us."

Griselda bit her lip. Then, with a sudden, disarming change of manner, she held out her hand to Jan.

"I know. I'm a beast—I told you I was," she said. "And, of course, I love Leslie. Only I know just what he's going to do and say all the time and it's too dreary for words. Then someone exciting and romantic comes along and I think what a mistake my marriage was and I wish everything was different and I suppose I do lose my head a bit. It's the way I'm made."

She sounded so complacent about it that Jan had a sudden desire to shake her and tell her that it was time she grew up and stopped being such an idiotic little nincompoop, but that would turn Griselda completely away from her, so she said, "I expect the 'someone romantic' would turn out to be just as dull by the time you'd been married to him long enough to know what *he* was going to do and say. You can't have it both ways."

But Griselda was no longer willing to talk. She drawled, "Listen to Teacher! You know all about marriage, I suppose!" and started to make up her face with care.

Jan turned towards the door, but before she reached it, Griselda called out, "All right, Jan, I'll be good, but don't try to make yourself out so disinterested about it all. At least I'm not a mercenary little gold-digger!"

Jan turned round, her hand on the door-knob. She would have liked to treat those words with a haughty indifference, but indignation and curiosity were too much for her.

"What do you mean?" she demanded.

Griselda's face was blank and innocent. She was running the tip of one finger along a delicate, black eyebrow and looking at it critically in the looking-glass. She spoke absently.

"Oh, you can't pretend you don't know that Luis is one of the richest men in these parts," she said mildly, but with an underlying note of spite. "Everyone has been watching you trying to catch him. A fiancé is easy enough to get rid of, and your stuffy barrister friend has only himself to blame if he loses you. Only I don't think marriage enters into Luis' calculations. I wonder what your boy-friend at home would say if he heard how you'd been dangling after bigger fish! Even Nick would be angry, you know. He has very strict ideas about how his family and employees should behave, and there's quite a lot I could tell both him and your Roderick. Think about it, my dear."

She began to apply lipstick, seeming to lose interest. Jan colored with rage and used all her self-control to restrain herself from shaking Griselda.

"How—how dare you talk such nonsense?" she demanded.

Griselda shrugged her shoulders.

"Is it nonsense?" she asked. "No one else thinks so."

Jan was speechless. She was aware suddenly that the girl she had liked and protected had become her enemy, and, ridiculous though her story was, a warning rang in Jan's head. Ridiculous—but Griselda could make it dangerous if she chose. Jan walked out of the cabin without a word, because she did not trust herself to speak.

CHAPTER THREE

ALTHOUGH, NEXT DAY, Griselda appeared to be exactly the same as usual, the little scene remained in Jan's mind, niggling a reminder whenever she spoke to Luis and leaving an unpleasant taste in her mouth. Thank goodness, she thought, that very soon they would be reaching Jamaica, and once on Dream Island she would be too busy to think any more about either Luis or Griselda's jealousy!

They were to dock early in the morning at Kingston, and Jan was up at crack of dawn to see her first sight of a new land. The sun was hot on her head even through her hat of fine straw, and she shaded her eyes with her hand to look at the distant shore—the glowing green of the foreground with the far-off blue sheen of half-seen mountains behind. Jan stayed by the rails, entranced, as they neared the quay and she saw the crowds waiting. The noise, the color, the glare were all so unlike anything she had ever known that she could scarcely take her eyes away.

Griselda came on deck, her brows drawn together in a peevish frown.

"I did think you would come and help me, Jan." she complained. "You know what a muddle my things get into! I just don't know how to put them straight."

Jan sighed. She would have liked to stay on deck to watch, but if she did nothing to put things right for Griselda, they would probably never get ashore at all! So she reassured her with, "All right! I'll see to things," and hurried down to Griselda's cabin.

By the time she had finished, visitors had come aboard. She stood for a moment, feeling rather alone because everyone else had someone there. At last she made out Griselda, chatting away to Leslie, her hand through his arm, her eyes adoring him as though she had never had any other thought while she had been away from him. He was grinning proudly down at her, his face a picture of happiness. Nicolas stood a little aloof, interested, and yet, somehow, apart from them and from Griselda's frivolous chatter. For a bare second Jan watched his strong profile, the clever eyes and firm mouth, and decided once more that she was glad to have him as her employer. Then, before she was able to make her way towards them, Luis detached himself from a small crowd which seemed to be holding a "welcome home" meeting round him and came towards her.

"This is where our paths divide," he said. "Griselda tells me you're going to Dream Island by the monthly steamer, leaving tomorrow. I'm flying straight there in a friend's private plane. So I'll be there before you. But I hope I'll be seeing you in a few days. This has been a good trip, hasn't it? For the first time for years, I haven't been bored."

"It's been my first trip anywhere, so I was very far from bored," she answered him. "Yes, I've enjoyed it very much, but don't expect to see much of me in Dream Island. I'll be too busy, I hope, to have time for anything else."

"Nonsense!" He laughed at her. "You don't think I'd let that happen, do you?"

She stiffened a little, resenting his proprietorial air. "You won't have much chance," she told him. "And now I really must go. I see Dr. Duncarron coming along here to fetch me."

She held out her hand to him, scarcely looking at him, because her eyes were now on Nicolas, striding towards her. She started to smile at him, but even before the smile was properly formed, Luis not only caught hold of her hand, but dragged her by it towards him.

She was taken completely unawares. She had had no idea of what he intended to do, and when he pulled her to him and, bending his head, kissed her thoroughly and lingeringly on the lips, she was so taken aback that, for a moment, she could not resist him.

At last she managed to pull herself away, angrier than she had been for a very long time.

"How—how could you?" she stammered. "You—you know there's nothing of that sort between us and to do it in front of everyone!"

Words here failed her. She was crimson in the face and

shaking with rage, but Luis tipped his handsome head backwards and laughed.

"I want everyone to know you have honored me with your friendship," he told her. "And you are sweet, my little Jan, so very sweet. Do not be angry with me."

"But I am—I'm absolutely furious!" she told him, and, seeing that further words would be completely wasted on him, she turned on her heel and moved away.

Nicolas had taken a step back. He could not possibly have missed seeing that unfortunate kiss, she thought miserably, and noticing the almost contemptuous coldness which had replaced his former friendly welcome, her heart sank. What a start to make in her new job!

"I'm sorry if I interrupted," he said distantly, when he had greeted her without any marked enthusiasm. "But it's time we went ashore. Griselda and Leslie have gone on."

"You didn't interrupt," she said, seeing herself in his eyes, a girl who could not even remain faithful to her fiancé for a couple of weeks. Anger with Luis was mixed with the helpless feeling of being misjudged; Nicolas knew nothing of her and would be likely to form his opinion of her from that unfortunate episode, especially if Griselda dropped her jealous hints into his ear. Jan could not help going on, "I didn't know he was going to kiss me, I didn't want him to."

"You needn't try to justify yourself to me," he told her. "It's none of my business how you say good-bye to your friends."

She thought she detected a touch of contempt in his voice and wished that she had said nothing. A dignified silence would have been better, but when you were all worked up with anger and a sense of injustice, both silence and dignity are difficult to maintain. She did her best to make up for her lapse now by following him with her head held high in the air and what she hoped was an expression of complete indifference on her face, but when they reached the Customs shed Griselda shattered even this by remarking, "Oh, there you are, Jan. I thought I'd be kind and leave you to say good-bye to Luis Corando on your own. Jan has been so friendly with our great neighbor all the trip," she amplified to Leslie. "She made quite a hit in that direction."

Leslie scowled.

"Is that rotter coming back to Dream Island?" he asked. "Sorry, Jan, if he's a friend of yours, but I don't like his methods—or himself much, for that matter."

"He's not a particular friend of mine," Jan answered awkwardly, hating the position she was being pushed into, unable through loyalty to make a come-back by revealing that Griselda had been just as much of a friend.

Griselda gave a short laugh, as though to say, "I could tell quite another tale!" and pressed Jan's hand, whispering just loud enough for the others to hear, "Never mind, darling; I won't tell tales out of school!"

Jan turned towards her luggage which had just been brought into the shed. She could not—she simply could not—look at Nicolas to see the expression on his face; she did not need to; she could imagine the somewhat fastidious scorn only too well.

Ever afterwards, Jan was unable to look back upon that brief stay in Jamaica without the bitterness of humiliation returning to her. She would have loved a country so new and so beautiful if things had been different; she would have revelled in the comforts of the Myrtle Bank Hotel. But, every time she relaxed, Griselda came out with a sweet, smiling remark which turned everything into dust and ashes, as far as Jan was concerned.

"Oh, Jan, you're looking quite pale!" Griselda exclaimed when they were alone. "You didn't really mind my teasing you, did you? That was all it was, you know."

"Yes, I did mind—very much," Jan answered flatly. "I don't know whether my sense of humour has gone wrong, but it doesn't seem funny to me to put me in such a bad light with my boss when he hasn't had a chance to find out for himself what I'm like. From the way everyone has been behaving, he must think me an empty-headed, flirtatious fool, and I don't blame him either!"

The corners of Griselda's mouth turned down as though she were about to cry.

"Oh, Jan, I never thought!" she cried repentantly. "I just wanted to get a teeny-weeny bit of my own back. But I wouldn't really hurt you for the world; you know that, don't you? I tell you what, I'll go straight to Nick and tell him nothing was your fault at all."

"No, you won't," Jan told her hastily. "You'll only make the importance of it all sound exaggerated. Just let things drop and don't keep giving hints, as if you could tell a lot of things if you wanted to, that's all."

"I won't say a single word!" Griselda's eyes became huge and as green as a cat's as she gazed at Jan with an ingenuousness that was much too good to be true. "But please don't be cross with me; I should just hate that."

Jan gave up. She did not know how far to believe in Griselda's repentance, but already far too much prominence had been given to the affair and the sooner it was dropped altogether the better. Soon they would be at Dream Island, and when Nicolas and she were working together at the hospital, he would be able to judge her work. And that, of course, was the only part of her that interested him.

They embarked on a tiny tramp steamer the following morning very early and had already sailed before seven o'clock. They were due to reach Dream Island by nightfall, after which the little ship would go on to others of the tiny, scattered islands, scarcely large enough to be included in a map.

It was a glorious day. The sun was a golden sheen on the intense blue of the sea, making so bright a path along it that even to look at it dazzled the eyes unbearably. After a while, Nicolas called Jan into the shade.

"You'll have to be careful of sunstroke now," he warned her. "Besides, it gets far too hot there. Come and sit down in the shade here while we discuss your work. How are you feeling about it now? Nervous about the differences?"

"Not a bit—just longing to get down to things. I've had far too long a holiday already." In her relief that he seemed to have forgotten all about yesterday's contretemps, she grinned frankly at him.

He answered the smile.

"Well, it isn't often I hear people admit that they'll be glad a holiday's over," he answered. "I hope you'll feel th same once you've got down to work!"

They both laughed, not because he had said anything amusing, but, on Jan's part at least, because she was so glad that there now seemed nothing between them and he had not judged her by Griselda's hints and sneers.

"Oh, it's lovely!" she cried suddenly in sheer joy of life. "The heat and the sun and the—the lushness of everything and all the smiling, colored faces and—well, everything."

He was serious now.

"That's what I feel like," he admitted. "But the tropics aren't all beauty, you know. There are things like snakes and scorpions. And, even worse, I think, frayed nerves and tempers that suddenly give way."

She wondered what he was thinking about. His face had become thoughtful and withdrawn and she had the feeling that, even though he was talking to her, he was thinking of someone else altogether.

Griselda, coming up at that moment, interrupted their talk, and soon afterwards a gong rang for lunch. After which, Nicolas insisted that everyone should have a siesta.

"You'll have to get into the way of it out here," he told Jan firmly when she protested that she neither needed nor wanted one. "Even if you don't sleep. It's too hot during the midday hours to go on as if you were at home. You'll only knock yourself up."

So, with one thing and another, their talk about the hospital never came off, and by the time they all collected on deck again Dream Island was showing, a green smudge against the blue and gold of the horizon.

Nicolas came to stand by Jan's side as the speck turned into a line which gradually assumed shape and depth and, from that, turned to a recognizable piece of land.

"Home," he said with satisfaction. "Wait a minute and you'll be able to make out the house."

She was standing on tiptoe in her excitement, and when he handed her some glasses she peered through them eagerly. A small pier was built to run out into the sea; it gleamed with a whiteness that seemed almost silver. On either side the sands were gold and studded with the pink transparency of tiny shells. A path cut sharply up the cliff to the land above and, gazing around her on all sides, Jan could make out long fields of a sharp, tall plant with spear-like leaves which she decided must be sugar-cane, and others where fruit trees clustered together with the gleam of the forming fruit upon them.

"It's so peaceful!" she murmured beneath her breath, and then turned the glasses towards the house he pointed out.

She could make it out quite clearly. A long, low pink-washed bungalow surrounded by a verandah and with a massed profusion of brilliant creepers twining up the walls and splashing the house with color. In front of it, a small garden was a blaze of blues and reds and oranges, dazzling in the sun. At a short distance from the house a long wooden building, unpainted and bare, made an incongruous note among the gracious loveliness of the house and its surroundings.

"That's the hospital," said Nicolas, pride touching his voice; then he looked down at her and laughed.

"I can just see you thinking, 'That a hospital! What on earth have I let myself in for'?" he told her.

She shook her head. He had not been very far off the mark. She had not felt dissatisfied, but she had for a moment, wondered however they could carry on in a building like that. But, almost at once, she began to imagine what fun it would be to start at the very beginning and to carry out improvements together. If Nicolas would allow them to work together and not only give her orders, and, somehow she thought he would.

She turned to smile her enjoyment at him, but the bustle on shore made her leave her words unsaid. They had reached the end of the white pier now and the boat was being made fast to it. A dozen negroes seemed to have appeared from nowhere to give their help, and the sound of their chattering voices and the sight of their smiling faces, teeth white and gleaming, took all her interest.

Griselda came up to them, waving to some of the people on shore.

"There's George," she said. "He's our gardener. And there's Lily—our housemaid. And——" She broke off to say in an amused tone, "Hello! What's this? Sarah-Ann—and hasn't she grown up since I've been away!"

Jan looked in the direction of her pointing finger. A girl was coming running down the cliff path, loose stones sliding beneath her feet in her haste. She took the last few feet at a jump and sprinted along the pier towards the small steamer. She was small and slender, in the briefest of pale green lined shorts with a boyish matching shirt. Her legs were bare and tanned, and her feet thrust into white sandals; her platinum blonde hair was tied back in a pony-tail that bumped up and down as she ran. But her face was charming—sun-tanned, with intensely blue eyes shaded by long lashes so dark as to be almost black.

Griselda took a step forward as the girl ran on board.

"Why, Sarah-Ann, how nice of you to come and meet us," she began.

But Sarah-Ann looked at her as though she did not see her, and, passing her, caught hold of Nicolas' arm.

"Oh, Nick, darling!" she cried. "It's seemed such ages since you went away! I've been on the look-out for you all day and then Dad called me away for something and I almost missed you! Don't forget we're going out tomorrow—you promised me!"

"I'm quite sure I didn't," he protested. "Not when Jan's just come and I've got to show her everything. But come along and be introduced."

He took her arm and propelled her unwillingly towards the others grouped together. Sarah-Ann's face had grown sulky, and the sparkling excitement had changed to the pettishness of a spoilt child. But she clung possessively to Nicolas' arm and Griselda looked from one to the other with open amusement.

"Well, Sarah-Ann," she repeated, "you *have* grown up while I've been away! Grown up so much that you didn't even recognize me when I spoke to you."

"I'm sorry, Mrs. Duncarron," Sarah-Ann apologized. "Of course I hadn't forgotten you. I was just so excited about seeing Nick again that I couldn't think of anything else. But you're quite right about one thing. I am grown up now—quite grown up. Aren't I, Nick?"

And she turned to regard Nicolas with a mixture of defiance and entreaty. Nicolas' eyes smiled indulgently and affectionately back at her. So that was it, Jan thought with such suddenness of surprise that it was like a blow. Nicolas and this lovely, child-like girl! Her breath came in a gasp of amazement.

CHAPTER FOUR

BUT, HOWEVER READY Jan might be to like Sarah-Ann, it was only too obvious that Sarah-Ann did not like her. The glance in which suspicion was mixed with distrust was only too obvious, and she put her hands behind her back with a quick, childish gesture, lost on Nicolas, who was not watching her, but noticed with delight by Griselda.

"Nick told me he was bringing a nurse here," Sarah-Ann said carefully. "But I expect you'll be terribly busy, won't you? I mean, there's so much to do on an island like this. You wouldn't believe how often the men cut themselves with their machetes and things like that, and I suppose you'll look after them."

Griselda chuckled and threw a glance at Nicolas, whose back was now turned to them as he superintended the unloading of the luggage.

"It's all right, Sarah-Ann," she told her in a conspiratorial whisper. "Jan's got two young men already, so unless she's the sort who goes about grabbing everyone she sees, you're quite safe with Nicolas."

Sarah-Ann crimsoned.

"I'm not jealous," she said with an attempt at dignified contempt. "Nicolas and I understand each other."

Whereupon she turned and walked up to him. Jan saw him look at her with that same gleam of affection and tolerance, and again she found herself wondering whether he was really half in love with the girl—or even more. Jan had not seen her at her best today; she was too transparently jealous of anything and anyone that took Nicolas' attention away from her after his absence from the island. But when she was not all prickles, she might well be a very charming companion. She was certainly a very pretty one.

Griselda watched her and laughed again.

"Absurd child!" she remarked in a tone that showed quite clearly her unfavourable opinion of Sarah-Ann. "But men are such fools. When you get a pretty face and a worshipping way that makes them feel big and heroic, they're likely to fall for the most extraordinary people!"

Then her tone changed and she added, "I'm so tired. I'm longing to get home. Why doesn't Leslie come and look after me? Oh, there's Lily. You know, I pointed her out before. She'll help me up the cliff if my husband won't bother."

The dark-skinned girl came up to them, grinning broadly.

"Glad you'se back, Mistress," she said. "We sure are all glad to see you. The Master said you wasn't so well."

"I'm not at all well, Lily," Griselda began in a complaining tone, but Lily said reassuringly, "It's that nasty cold country, Mistress. You'll be all right now you're back home with us. Let me help you up home. There's some supper all awaiting for you there."

Griselda submitted to being helped up the steep cliff, making much heavier weather of it than Jan privately thought necessary when she remembered all the exercise she had taken on board ship. Lily, however, seemed to take it all as a matter of course, and, putting one bit of conversation on to another, Jan began to realize that Griselda adopted the role of semi-invalid on Dream Island. She frowned. What, she wondered, would be the best way to pull her out of that idea? Already, she was beginning to see that her work was going to be well cut out for her.

The bungalow was cool and fresh, with long, high rooms, palely painted to give an effect of coolness. Mosquito netting covered the front of the verandah to make it an extra living-room—in fact, as Jan learnt, it was used far more than any of the other rooms. Lily, who first saw Griselda to her room and then took charge of Jan, told her proudly that electricity was made from their own private plant and water pumped up to the house.

"When I was a little girl and the old Mr. Duncarron came to live here, there was nothing," she said, a proprietorial pride in her voice. "Jus' a little ol' wooden shack with kerosene lamps to light it and water pumped up from the ol' well at the end of the garden. An' now we've everything —nearly as smart as that Mas'r Corando, and he's a millionaire. My masters aren't that. After all, who wants to have all that money for himself? Dr. Nicolas could never be a millionaire 'cause he gives far too much away—more than he can afford, Mistress says. But isn't it better that way?"

Jan agreed that it was. The Duncarrons certainly had a devoted champion in their housemaid. It was quite evident that they could do no wrong in her eyes. Even the fact that they were not overburdened with this world's goods seemed a point in their favour.

"There's trouble, though," Lily went on angrily. "Not us—we in the island know the Duncarrons and we've sense enough to know when we're lucky. It's the outsiders; talking of striking and I don't know what. We don't want that sort of thing on our island, we told them straight. If you leave your own land and come to another, you must do as the people you've come to do. That's right, isn't it? But they say we don't know what we're talking about. That Ben Grant—just because I ain't never left Dream Island. Well, and I don't want to if I'll meet people with manners like yours on the other islands, I told him straight out. We don't want none of them nasty ways."

Jan was trying to disentangle this when a voice from the regions in the rear of the house called Lily and she ran off. Evidently, Jan decided, Nicolas and Leslie had engaged some workmen from the other islands and they were demanding more payment and threatening strike action. It spoilt the idyllic peace of the place a little, but Jan believed that the two Duncarrons were very well able to manage things themselves—as well as, quite obviously, being extremely popular on the island.

There was something about the place, she thought, as she awoke next morning. She felt as though she had been here for years already; as though some part of her belonged. She had fallen asleep to the ceaseless whirr of crickets, to the strange tropical rustlings and movements of the still night air, to distant barking of dogs and braying of donkeys, to the far-off, scarcely-heard sound of drums and a strummed guitar. She awoke to the brilliant warmth of sunlight, to the triumphant crowing of a persistent cock and the screech of a gaudily colored bird.

She jumped up to look out of her window. There was a splash of vivid blue against the brown of a tree trunk just outside; as she watched, it moved with a quick slither of color to vanish from her sight and she realized that it must have been an iguana. A small brown lizard was curled contentedly on a corner of her wall; she remembered hearing that they kept down mosquitoes and left it where it was. Then she dressed quickly in the plain white frock with neat collar and cuffs which would make a practical, neat and cool uniform for this climate.

Breakfast of coffee, rolls and fruit was served on the verandah, where Leslie and Nicolas were already seated. Jan eyed the variety of fruit with interest. Oranges, grapefruit, paw-paw, sweet- and sour-sop, bananas, grapes, and others whose names she did not know.

"I hope you don't mind our starting without you," Nicolas said when he had asked how she slept. "Leslie and I have been riding round the estate and we're hungry. Work starts early in the tropics, while it's still cool."

She noticed, then, that they were both wearing white riding-suits and that broad-brimmed sombreros were hanging over a near-by chair.

"I feel horribly lazy," she admitted. "I'll get up earlier tomorrow. Is Griselda up yet?"

"Oh, no; she never gets up till lunch-time," Leslie told her in some surprise. "She isn't really fit for more."

Jan's lips set tightly as she remembered the nights Griselda had spent dancing, only to be up in the morning to walk round the deck with Luis before breakfast, but she said nothing. Time enough to have things out with Griselda when she had decided on the best way to treat her — for it was part of her work, she knew, to pull her into a more rational way of life. She had an idea, though, that Nicolas knew what she was thinking, for there was an understanding gleam in his eye as she met it.

"I'm holding a clinic at the hospital in about half an hour," was all he said, however. "Would you like to come along? We haven't any patients in it yet, of course, but I can show you round and you'll meet the people you'll be looking after. I want to have everything ready there in case we get a sudden emergency."

"Yes, please," Jan told him, her voice so eager that he smiled, and Leslie said quickly, "It's the first time Nick has had anyone to share his pet hobby-horse with him, so he'll probably keep you at it all the time."

"It's what I'm here for," Jan reminded him. "I'm all ready. Shall we go?"

"What enthusiasm!" Nicolas uncurled his long length slowly from his chair and reached for his sombrero. "You'd better wear a hat. You're not used to this sun."

It took Jan only a minute to fetch it, and soon they were crossing the well-watered lawn to the hut at the far end. It was an ideal position, shaded by trees, with a view in front of the stretch of blue sea and golden sands.

"I want to make a small flower garden in front where convalescent patients can sit," Nicolas explained. "And a kitchen one at the back to grow our own vegetables. There's still a tremendous amount to be done. But now you're here I'm much more hopeful about it all. You're the first person who hasn't just laughed at the idea and said it was quite impossible."

"But of course it isn't!" she exclaimed in shocked surprise, and repeated the remark several times as she saw over the hut.

It was larger than it looked from outside. A long central passage ran down the whole length. Just inside the door was a room which acted both as Nicolas' office and surgery. From the passage, four doors opened off to disclose wards, each of which already contained four narrow iron beds, their mosquito nets already put up, and everything ready to be made up quickly if necessary. Two somewhat primitive bathrooms were at the end of the passage, and a second door led to a small separate kitchen away from the hospital itself. A second shed was to be the operating-theatre one day, though at present it contained only the table and instruments he had brought back from England with him.

Jan compared it silently with the huge efficient power of her hospital at home, and quite suddenly this pathetic, hopeful bit of the future gave a quick tug of protective love at her heart and she knew that ever afterwards she would regard it with an affection that no modern hospital with every new invention and stream-lined efficiency could rouse in her.

She became aware suddenly that Nicolas was watching her anxiously.

"I hadn't realized it was so terribly primitive until I started to see it through your eyes," he said at last. "And you straight from St. Francis! If you want to go home at once I shan't blame you!"

"But I don't." She turned on him such a look of surprise that he could not mistake her earnestness. "It's going to be such fun for us, getting everything going together!"

His face lit up quickly.

"Partners, are we?" he asked. "Here's to the firm of Duncarron and Lorrimer!'

He held out his hand, laughing, but, even as she put hers into his, he dropped it hastily.

"But I forgot," he said, his voice changing. "There won't be a firm for long, will there? You'll be getting married in a few months and that'll be the end of your work out here."

Jan looked at him, surprised by his sudden change of manner.

"Not as soon as all that," she told him. "There'll be time to get things going."

Her words were interrupted by a call of, "Duncarron! Are you there, Duncarron?" and both of them wheeled round.

Luis Corando was walking along the corridor with an easy swing that made him look almost as if the place belonged to him. His white suit was immaculate; a crimson rose was still dew-splashed in his buttonhole. His gaze took in Nicolas' shabby riding-kit as he said, "You're one of the world's workers, I can see — up at dawn to start your toil. I must apologize for interrupting you."

His look passed to Jan and he bowed as he went on, "Jan, my dear. As sweet and fresh as ever. I see I must become ill so that you can look after me! You're not going to work her so hard, are you, Duncarron, that she'll have no time to go out with me? I've been looking forward to that all the time we were on our way here."

Nicolas stiffened. His voice was curt as he said, "Jan can do exactly as she wishes," and Jan wished with all her heart that Luis had not come to disturb them. Their closeness seemed to have been broken and she had a horrible feeling that it would take a long time for it to return.

She was going to say that she did not want to go out with him, when he said suavely, "Can I see you on a matter of business, Duncarron?"

He turned to Jan to add, "I know that you will understand that business must come before pleasure, my dear."

Jan hated him so much for the lowered tone of intimacy in his voice that she answered sharply, "I've got business as well as you, and it will keep me busy here all the time. It's my pleasure too."

But she did not think that either of them heard her. Nicolas' face had grown hard and his voice was harsh as he said, "If the business is to do with the sale of our land, the answer is still the same, so it's no use discussing it."

Luis raised his eyebrows.

"Oh, but, my dear man, I think there is every use," he replied. "I beg you will hear me out. I think you will find it of the utmost importance to you."

Jan looked from one to the other and suddenly her heart sank. All the happy anticipation had gone out of the day, and as she watched the two tall men, one smiling but with an unyielding determination beneath the suavity, the other openly hostile, she felt suddenly afraid. Afraid of what their mutual dislike — almost she called it enmity— might bring.

CHAPTER FIVE

NICOLAS BROKE THE silence by saying abruptly, "I can give you a few minutes, but not longer. I've got a clinic here then, and I don't intend to keep my patients waiting."

"Ah, yes, the hospital." Luis' eyes slid round the pitifully bare, shiningly clean building and his lips twitched a little as though the sight amused him. "A most praiseworthy idea and one that deserves encouragement. But you don't really think this place is going to do, do you? It's going to need a lot of money spent on it, you know."

"I'll manage." Nicolas ground out the words almost savagely. "But we're wasting time. If you'll come to the point—"

"That is the point—or part of it," Luis interrupted him. "I am interested in the hospital—very interested—and I should like to help."

Nicolas looked an astonished question, at the sight of which Luis laughed softly.

"And why not?" he asked. "Why should I not be as interested in the welfare of my workmen as you are in yours? And, without boasting, I think I may say that I have a great deal more money than you are ever likely to have."

Nicholas' brows drew together darkly as he watched him, his eyes wary.

"Is there a string attached?" he asked at last.

"A string?" Luis shrugged elegant shoulders. "That is to put it bluntly. No, not exactly what you call a string. Of course, we should need to go into the matter with great care. You would probably have to make it a full-time job. There is so much we could do. A properly organized health centre, maternity clinic, child welfare — oh, a multitude of things! Jan would need help too. Two or three nurses. We could make it a little model — a small gem of perfection."

Nicolas' expression did not relax.

"You never do anything for nothing," he reminded Luis.

"Who does?" Luis wanted cheerfully to know. "Now, look here, my dear fellow, let's talk sense. Things are changing, as you, a man of intelligence, must know. The day of the small landowner is done. The companies and combines are able to undercut him all round. They can run things at so much cheaper a rate and have so much greater capital behind them that the individual simply cannot compete. It is sad, but it is the way of the world. A hurricane — an earthquake — a run of bad luck — and poof! It is all gone. Bankruptcy for anyone who has no backing. That is why I am suggesting — as much for your good as my own, though I do not pretend to be a philanthropist — that you should concentrate all your great gifts on this hospital. If you sell me your estate, your brother could remain on as manager, and your so-charming sister-in-law, if she wished to stay out here, could still have the bungalow, and we could all be happy. I am talking sense, no?"

His foreign accent intensified itself towards the end of his speech as though he were not quite as confident as he wished to sound. Nicolas had listened to him in silence; now he was standing motionless, but to Jan, watching him from the distance to which she had removed herself, his tautness hinted at a strain, a violence held in check with difficulty.

When he spoke, his voice was as expressionless as his face.

"You're a cunning devil, aren't you, Corando?" he asked. "You know just where to apply the pressure. Almost like blackmail."

"Blackmail?" Luis' voice was pained. "There is no comparison. I am only suggesting a solution that may appeal to everyone."

Jan caught the words as his voice rose, and was carried back to that day on board ship when she had accused Luis of a kind of blackmail and he had answered in almost the same manner. Yes; he was certainly very clever. She wondered whether the Duncarrons with their downright honesty would be any match for him.

"Look here, Luis went on, still talking in an exaggeratedly reasonable tone. "I get what I want. I always have. It is the secret of my success. But you are my friends, I hope. I want you to get what, in the long run, you will want, too, even if you don't want it now. You can't last much longer, you know, dear chap. Already there is discontent among your workers. They want more pay and you can't afford to give it to them. Later there will be real trouble. But I can afford higher pay—"

"Did you put them up to this?" Nicolas interrupted harshly. "Is it a plan to get rid of us?"

Luis withdrew a little in affronted dignity, his eyes filled with shocked horror, yet Jan could not quite feel that his surprise was genuine, skilfully acted though it must be if not.

"I think you do not quite know what you are accusing me of," he said slowly. "I refuse to take offence because I will not believe that you mean what you say. Now I will leave you. I do not ask for a decision from you straight away. Think it over. Only I beg you to remember how much good you will be doing the people here if we work the hospital together. And I think you might remind Leslie that if he agrees, he, as a married man, will have no more need to worry about crops and prices. Whatever happens, he will have money—plenty of money—to support his wife. On the other hand, if you refuse, I can scarcely be expected to take such an interest in the hospital or give to it so freely. While your brother will have many worries. He will, too, be much busier than he would be as my manager, and his wife will continue to be lonely and bored — unless I can find some amusement for her."

He turned to look straight at Jan as he spoke the last words. She and she alone knew that they constituted a threat. To Nicolas, knowing nothing of what had happened on board ship, they would sound merely a friendly offer of help. Jan knew otherwise and her heart gave a leap of alarm. She could not trust Griselda not to lose her head if Luis did make it his business to run after her.

Luis, with his infallible sense of the most telling curtain, raised his hand in salute, bowed to Jan and saying, "Now

I will keep you no longer from your so-impatient clinic," strode gracefully away without waiting for an answer.

Not that Nicolas seemed to have any to give. He was looking at nothing with a particular intensity, black brows drawn into an anxious bar. At last, he strengthened himself with a worried sigh.

"The devil of it is he's so infernally clever," he said, and she thought that he was speaking aloud to himself rather than consciously to her. "He has caught us both in a web—the two things that matter most to both of us. Have I any right to deprive the islanders of all he can give them? I can't pretend to compete. Before he started to talk, I'd thought my own hopes so fine, but now they're just pathetically absurd. And has Leslie the right to keep security from Griselda? You know how much all the conventional signs of prosperity mean to her. And I'll admit that we're walking a tightrope at present. We've enough money to keep going if things go on as they have been doing the last few years. The men have been paid a fair rate of pay—as much as any other owners give them and various bonuses as well—but if wages are going to be pushed up, and if there's a hurricane or an earthquake or anything of that sort, it means that we fall off the rope and have to start right from the beginning again, with lots of bumps and bruises to hinder us. And yet, Golden Grove—"

He broke off, walking to the end of the corridor and leaning against the door, so that his eyes swept the great expanse of land before them, the fields glowing in the sunlight, the flowers a many-hued halo of beauty against the green trees and warm brown of the earth. Jan followed him rather uncertainly. She did not know whether, in his absorption, he realized that she was there at all, and she did not want the awkwardness of making him aware he had spoken so freely to a comparative stranger if he had been too taken up in his own thoughts to appreciate the fact.

But his perplexed face, his worried frown and something almost desperate in its longing as he gazed at his land made her want to comfort him. She wanted, suddenly, to put her hand on his arm and to tell him that she understood and wanted to help him. But, of course, she could not do that. Instead, she said quietly, "Does Golden Grove mean a lot to you?"

He started and looked at her for the first time as though he were really seeing her. Then he smiled wryly.

"I must be boring you stiff," he apologized. "I'm sorry."

"But you're not," she protested. "I'm interested. If you don't think I'm being nosy."

He shook his head.

"You're one of us now," he reminded her. "But I don't know whether you would understand our feeling for the estate. When we came out here, it was a wilderness. We hadn't the money to employ a lot of men, so we set to ourselves to put it in order. We'd never been in the tropics before and we'd never done any farming, but we worked from dawn till dark almost without stopping. We were usually too tired to do more than stagger home and throw ourselves down on our beds. In the morning we ached in every inch, and during the day in the fierceness of the heat we felt as though all our strength was being sweated out of us. But then luck came our way. We had three good harvests in succession. We were able to employ workers; Leslie went home and married Griselda, and we made the house nice for her. Things are very different now from the old days, of course, but the effect remains. When you've suffered over anything, when it has been an agony and a joy and a worry that eats into your bones, it becomes part of you, rooted in you. Can you understand that? Guess perhaps it's what a woman feels when her child is born. Golden Grove is our child—made by us, the result of pain and worry and yet happiness. We have put down our roots into the soil in which we sowed the cane and the fruit trees, and it has become part of us. To hand it over to someone who would only think of it as another piece of land to help to make him even richer, to be employees on the place that means so much to us——"

He broke off, reddening.

"I'm sorry," he apologized. "What must you think of me, talking like that? It sounds so—so idiotic."

"It sounds real and true and I know how you must feel," she told him. "But you haven't decided to sell it yet, have you?"

He shook his head.

"Les and I will have to talk it over," he said. "We'd have refused, both of us, if he hadn't caught us on our weak spot. And he knows it. I suppose I'm being libellous, but I believe that this sudden wage claim is engineered by him. There has always been such a happy feeling on the estate before."

He broke off, looking at her ruefully.

"I keep on putting my foot in it this morning," he went on. "I'd forgotten Corando and you were such friends. You must be furious with me for what I've said about him."

"But I'm not," she assured him. "We're not such friends. He's an amusing companion, but——"

She had a sudden desire to tell him everything, to let him know that she trusted Luis no more than he did, that, if he did not get what he wanted, he might make serious trouble between Leslie and Griselda. Nicolas might know what to do in that direction.

But he seemed suddenly to have withdrawn from her, as though he regretted his expansiveness and, while she was trying to frame the right words, Sarah-Ann came running across the grounds towards the hospital.

"I heard you were going to have your first clinic here today," she called out as she ran, long, beautiful legs flying, hair tossing up and down on her shoulders. "I came to see if I could help. I know I'm not clever like Jan, but I can hand things and help to look after the children. I'd love to, really."

Nicolas regarded her with an amused and affectionate gleam in his eye.

"This is something new," he teased her. "Sure you really mean to work? Because I'm a regular slave-driver, and if you start to help you'll have to keep at it and not run off as soon as it bores you."

She nodded her head emphatically.

"I've decided that I'm a parasite," she told him solemnly. "It's time I did something to justify my existence. And I really am good at all the odd jobs, you know. And if I watch you and Jan very hard, perhaps I'll learn enough to go on to more interesting ones. Please."

Her tone was appealing. He laughed again and answered, "O.K., I'll take you at your word. Come on, then. And you, too, Jan. The clinic ought to have opened half an hour ago, so, allowing for everyone's idea of time out here, they ought to be starting to arrive."

He started to walk towards the office. Sarah-Ann pushed her hand into his arm and skipped along by his side, talking twenty to the dozen. Jan felt curiously deflated. The time for confidences was past. She could not discuss Griselda with him now and she wondered, with a sinking of her heart, whether there would ever be another chance or whether he had really put her on the side of Luis and regretted his earlier expansiveness.

CHAPTER SIX

A CHEERFUL BUZZ OF conversation came to their ears as they neared the office. Nicolas pushed the door open to disclose half a dozen proud mothers with their offspring. Jan caught her breath at the sight of the sheer beauty of the negro babies with their huge, velvety black eyes and the soft sheen of their skins.

But there was little time for her to look at them now. The mothers were all crowding round Nicolas with exclamations of delight, and when he introduced her to them as their nurse, they transferred their attention to her, touching her uniform, giggling with delight, remarking candidly and surprisingly touchingly about the color of her hair and the fairness of her complexion. Sarah-Ann was forgotten until she said in a loud voice, "I thought this was a medical clinic, Nick, not an admiration society."

Nicolas grinned at her.

"Kittens shouldn't show their claws, you know," he said in a low tone, though his smile was tolerant. All the same, he clapped his hands and restored order to the room.

After that, the scene might almost have taken place in a hospital at home. Jan watched Nicolas without seeming to do so, and she approved of his sure, gentle touch, his reassuring manner and his evident understanding of his patients. When they had all been attended to, he said, "That's all for today, but I want you all to bring your babies to me and Nurse once a month to be weighed and checked up. Nurse will go to your houses every now and again to see how everyone is going on. But I don't only want to look after the babies already born; I want to make sure that those who are going to be born will have a chance of coming into this world strong and healthy and that their mothers will have everything possible done to help them. So I want all expectant mothers to come to a monthly clinic, too. Will you tell everyone, and those of you who are expecting come as well? What about it Katy?"

The woman he spoke to wriggled and giggled.

"But we don't need no clinic, Dr. Nicolas," she told him. "It's natural to have children; we don't need no doctor to tell us it's happening."

"I'm sure you don't, but if you have a monthly check-up on your health, it will make sure that both you and the baby are going on well," he explained.

"Oh, I don't know." The women looked at each other uncertainly, giggling and shy. "Our menfolk won't want us to waste time that way."

"That's just too bad." Nicolas appeared to shelve the subject. "Because I meant to make quite a little party of it. Coffee and cakes and a gossip. But, of course, if it's a waste of time——"

"Go on with you, Doctor. You know we'll none of us miss a party," Katy told him, chuckling. "I'll tell everyone and we'll all be here."

Laughing and gossiping, they streamed out of the door. Jan smiled in sympathy; that was a clever touch of Nicolas', she thought; the one way of making sure of their attendance.

He turned away from the wash-basin at which he had been washing his hands as she told him so.

"This is only the beginning," he said. "When you get to know them and visit them in their houses as a trusted friend, there's a lot more I want you to do to help. The children's diet—that's all wrong, you know. Beans, rice, bananas and coffee. I want you to try to educate them in that. But it'll be slow work and will have to be carried out very carefully and by degrees. The water supply, too. Some of the wells they use are absolutely brackish. I always dread an outbreak of typhoid. But they say their fathers and mothers always used those wells, and what was good enough for them is good enough for their children. Oh, there's heaps to be done!"

He turned towards her, his face eager, all his previous anxieties apparently forgotten. Jan warmed to his enthusiasm. Besides, she liked the warm-hearted, friendly people; she was longing to become their friend, to visit them in their small thatched huts with the small, neat gardens round.

"Oh, yes, they're picturesque, I grant you that," Nicolas

answered when she said something about the huts. "But most of them are insanitary in the extreme. Still, we've made a start now and we'll make real progress once they adopt you as one of us."

Sarah-Ann, whose behaviour had been exemplary during the clinic, now regarded them with a frown. She began to fidget, toss her head and make small, interrupting noises which Nicolas, in his absorption, failed to notice. Sarah-Ann looked from him to Jan, evidently longing to break in, but afraid that she would meet with a snub. At last, however, her feelings became too much for her and she caught hold of Nicolas' arm, tilting her head back to look up at him with eyes appealing through long lashes.

"Nick, darling, I've been Florence Nightingale as long as you wanted," she reminded him. "I enjoyed it and I thought I was rather good. But now it's all over, can't we have fun? Aren't you going to ride round the estate, because my horse needs exercise terribly badly and it might be a good thing if I came with you. As a reward," she coaxed him.

"I went round the estate at six this morning," he told her. "Leslie's out there now. If you want a ride with me, you'll have to be up at dawn. Which, knowing your capacity for sleep, I think most unlikely. But you can come with Jan and me, if you like. I'm going to take her round the village to introduce her to everyone."

Sarah-Ann pulled a face.

"I wanted just you and me," she told him candidly. "But I expect it'll be very nice with Jan, too," she added hastily, as though she realized that open rudeness to Jan would get her nowhere.

They were about to start out when running footsteps were heard outside the hospital and a man came in, panting and hot from his haste.

"Sah, bad accident," he managed to bring out between labored breaths. "Mr. Leslie sent me to tell you. Bill White caught in tractor. Very bad. Mr. Leslie bringing him. He says he wants you to see him at once."

Nicolas asked some hurried questions but, quick though he was, he had barely finished them when Leslie and two other men came in, carefully carrying an unconscious and badly hurt man upon an improvised stretcher.

Bill White—who was the blackest islander Jan had yet seen—was unconscious. He had fallen under the tractor and one arm was crushed. Sarah-Ann gave a moan when she saw the blood and rushed outside, but no one noticed her absence. Nicolas seemed to be a different man as he took command, cutting away the sleeve and examining the wound.

"Looks like our first operation," he said, turning to Jan.

For a bare second, Jan panicked. Their first operation and nothing ready. Not even, as far as she knew, boiling water in which to sterilize the instruments. She thought fleetingly and longingly of her old hospital operating-theatre, of the shining cleanliness and asepticness, of all modern aids ready to hand, and she wondered whether she could ever manage here. If the man died through her negligence——

Then Nicolas spoke again, his eyes on her, searching her face, as though he could see the quickly scurrying beats of panic. "We can send him to one of the larger islands after I've given first aid if you don't think you can manage here yet. Luis still has his private plane here."

Jan closed her eyes for a bare second that seemed an eternity, from the number of thoughts that raced through her mind. Send him away! Subject him to delay, to danger of complications that might set in if he were not attended to at once! No; she knew she could not do that. By the time she had opened her eyes again, fear was under command.

"No; don't do that," she told Nicolas. "We'll manage."

"Good girl." His tone approved and told her he understood. "Run across to the house. Tell Lily to bring over boiling water—gallons of it if she can. I'm going to get things ready. You'll have to give the anaesthetic, I'm afraid. No one else to see to it."

Jan swallowed as she nodded. Words were beyond her. She did not know how she would face the ordeal ahead and yet she knew that she would do it. Somehow, it meant more than just the man's life, important though that was. The whole future of the hospital, the little, gallant, brave effort against so many odds, all sorts of things she scarcely understood yet, seemed at stake.

Luckily, there was no time for thought. She fetched boiling water; she sterilized the instruments; she scrubbed up and put on a long white overall and mask. Then, quite calmly, almost as though she were doing it in a dream, she stood by Nicolas' side, following his instructions as quickly and as competently as though his mind had extended itself to her, as though some invisible line stretched between them, carrying messages scarcely spoken.

She was able to notice his quickness and accuracy. Not a second wasted. His fingers moved, without noticeable hurry and yet surprisingly quickly and surely. He was, she realized an unusually skilled surgeon, and something like triumph soared within her and elation at being able to work with him.

It was over at last. Bill was taken to one of the wards and put into bed there. Nicolas peeled off his gloves with a sigh in which weariness and deep satisfaction were mixed.

"He'll do," he said. "Thanks to you. I shouldn't have blamed you if you'd panicked, but you were fine. Well, I've given you a patient before you've had time to turn round. Can you look after him now? I'll take over this evening and during the night if you're not too tired to manage till then."

"No; I want to," she replied. "I hadn't realized it could be so satisfying. It's wonderful in hospital when you have everything at your command. But here—with nothing—it's an indescribable feeling."

"I thought you'd understand." He looked absurdly pleased. "Come outside for a breath of fresh air."

He led her outside. She was almost surprised to find the sun still hot in the sky; it seemed as though hours must have passed since Bill White had been brought into the building. She pulled off her cap and ran her hand through her rumpled hair.

A middle-aged woman with greying hair, her dark face raddled with tears, came hurrying up and seizing Nicolas' hand, kissed it fervently.

"Thenk you, Dr. Nick," she said, sobs still rising in her throat. "You save my man. If he had been taken away, who knows what might have happened? And he so far from home and longing for the island which he's never left. Thank God for you, Doctor, and the hospital where you can make your own people well."

"I didn't do anything, Sophia," Nicolas assured her.

Sophia shook her head and walked off, to be surrounded almost at once by a crowd of her friends, ready to console and congratulate. Nicolas looked after them thoughtfully and then down at his hand.

"It's no use," he said suddenly. "I can't do it. Do you mind, Jan, if we don't have the fine hospital Luis has offered us? I can't hand things over to someone who doesn't care. I'm going to fight him—whatever happens."

CHAPTER SEVEN

SOMETHING IN NICOLAS' voice stirred enthusiasm in Jan. She turned to him with her eyes shining.

"I'm glad," she answered. "You're quite right. All these people—they know and trust you. They want your personal interest, not the impersonality of a proper hospital, however modern and wonderful it may be. Oh, I'm so glad."

Her delight could not be mistaken. Nicolas looked at her with an amused gleam in his eye.

"Even though it's Luis I'm fighting?" he asked.

"Oh, what has that to do with it? I'd say the same whoever it was." But her voice died away at the end on a note of uncertainty. It might matter; being Luis, she meant. Because of Griselda, because the infuriating and yet somehow lovable woman was not likely to keep her head where he was concerned, and, if he really wanted to get his own back that way, both Leslie and his wife were painfully vulnerable.

So she stopped short and Nicolas turned to give her a look that held both question and disappointment. She wondered whether he was remembering the kiss Luis had given her and the hints Griselda had thrown out, and, more than ever after today, when their victory in the hospital seemed to have formed a bond between them, she did not want him to think all the things Griselda had done her best to make them think.

Luis himself doesn't matter in the least to me," she began. "You forget I'm engaged."

"On the contrary, I have remembered it several times," he answered her gravely. "Quite frankly, I don't understand the relationship between you and Luis, but it isn't any of my business."

"But, in a way, it is," she began eagerly. "I'm not thinking of myself at all. But there are so many complications. I think I ought to tell you——"

He interrupted her quickly.

"Don't," he ordered. "Don't spoil what started out to be a red-letter day. The opening of the hospital, our first patient, the operation that went well when everything seemed against it. I want to be able to think of those things. Don't clutter them up with thoughts of Luis and his threats."

She became silent. She couldn't tell him about Griselda now. In any case, her feelings were too complex. Someone ought to be warned, but she would be giving away a confidence in telling the whole story, and enough of her schoolgirl code remained to give her a horror of betraying anyone else. So she said nothing, and as they stood there, the soft play of the warm breeze lifting her hair and ruffling her skirts against her legs, Sarah-Ann emerged from a house and came slowly towards them.

She came without any of her usual enthusiasm and bounce. Her face was very white and her eyes were rimmed with red as though she had been crying. She hung her head as she walked and scuffed her sandals in the dusty ground.

"I'm sorry, Nicolas," she said as she came near to them, her voice surprisingly humble. "I'm terribly ashamed of myself."

"What about, for goodness' sake, infant?" he asked. "I can't think of anything you have to be ashamed of yourself about."

"Because—because—when they brought Bill White in, I couldn't look," she confessed. "I just saw his arm and I ran out and was sick and I simply couldn't go back again."

He smiled a little, but his voice was serious as he answered, "Nothing very bad about that. You couldn't have helped—as a matter of fact, I hadn't even noticed that you'd gone."

She swallowed at that, looking so piteous that Jan felt a quick wave of sympathy and said, "It's quite usual for people to feel sick about things like that at first. Nurses often faint when they're first put on in the operating-theatre—and medical students, too. It's the sort of thing that takes time to get used to."

Nicolas grinned reminiscently.

"Did it myself," he confessed. "Never felt such a fool in my life. But one soon gets used to it."

"Do you?" Sarah-Ann's face lit up. "Do you really? Because I was thinking if you'd have me, I'd like to help. I mean, after today, I can't go round pretending I'm a born Florence Nightingale, but I could start with dusting and bedpans and, if you'd teach me—and if I really would get used to blood—I truly would like to help."

"I don't suppose we'll get as many bad accidents as all that," Nicolas answered. "And I'm sure Jan would be glad of help. But it's quite a different question whether you'd be able to stick it. Anyway, I'll go and see your father and talk it over with him."

"Come now," Sarah-Ann begged him. "I do mean it, really, and I'm not such a weakling that I can't stick a thing once I make up my mind."

"I'll go back to the patient," Jan put in. She knew that if Sarah-Ann had made up her mind to come to the hospital, Nicolas would not be able to refuse her. Jan would be glad of help, but she had her doubts as to whether anything useful would be forthcoming from Sarah-Ann unless Nicolas were about. So she left them to arrange matters among themselves while she went to sit by Bill White, who was now beginning to come round from the anaesthetic.

Nicolas did not tell her what Mr. Anderson's reactions had been when faced by the fact that his daughter had so suddenly decided that she was a parasite and wanted to become a nurse. Whatever it was, Sarah-Ann twisted him round her little finger as she had done all her life, and when Nicolas came over in the evening to take over from Jan, he informed her that she would have a new help the next day.

Nor did he tell her of his discussion with Leslie of Luis Corando's offer, nor whether he had been to see Luis to tell him of the result. After all, why should he? It was none of her business. All the same, he had discussed it with her at first, and had told her of the strength of his feelings for Golden Grove, and she could not help harbouring a slight disappointment that he did not think it worth telling her the outcome.

She had not much time for disappointment or any other feeling, however. Her time was taken up with such a rush of activity that anything unconnected with the hospital had to be pushed into the background. Bill White, with his magnificent constitution, was recovering at a greater speed that she had dared to hope, but that, in itself, made another problem. He had what seemed a whole regiment of relations—father, mother, wife, innumerable children and even more innumerable brothers and sisters, and they all wanted to visit him and cheer him up. It was quite impossible to make them realize that there should be special visiting hours. Jan printed a large and very black notice, bearing the words, VISITING HOURS, 2—3 AND 7—8 P.M. DAILY. This was a matter of extreme interest to the visitors, who made their children spell it out to show how well their reading was progressing, but that was where the matter ended. They continued to walk into the hospital at any odd hour between 6 a.m. and 11 p.m. with blandly smiling, innocent faces and, in the end, in despair Jan turned the notice round with its face to the wall.

Although Bill remained the only patient, Jan made it a rule to spend a certain amount of time every day visiting the village huts and getting to know everyone. They were all—or almost all—most friendly, but she sensed a certain reserve amongst them and a most decided disinclination to carry out her suggestions.

"They don't know you yet," Nicolas told her. "Give them a little time and they'll adopt you as one of themselves. They like you already and that's something. If they hadn't, you wouldn't have got anywhere with them."

So Jan decided upon patience. It was difficult enough when her enthusiasm was at white heat and she was longing to start all the health reforms so badly needed. But already she was learning that haste did not pay in this land of tropical sun and languor.

The exception to the general friendliness was the small group of men who had come from other islands to work at Golden Grove and the other two estates. Watching their sullen faces and grumbling voices, so unlike the lovely lilt of the islanders, Jan could not help wondering whether Luis could somehow have brought over regular trouble-makers for some devious reason of his own. Otherwise, it seemed hard to understand their attitude; she soon found out that they were receiving a most generous rate of pay and could not have been treated with more consideration anywhere.

So her days were busy. Sarah-Ann appeared at the hospital each day, wearing a tailor-made white overall with her primrose-yellow hair adorned by a wisp of lace she called a cap. But after the first day she spent most of her time curled up in a chair in Jan's sitting-room, poring over a glossy magazine, and came to life only when Nicolas was there or when a clinic was being held.

Jan found that invitations were awaiting her from all the houses on the island. The Andersons' pleasant, unpretentious bungalow; the little white wooden hut occupied by Garth Owen, Luis' manager, who turned out to be a good-natured, sandy-haired and freckled young man; Luis' own large, castle-like home, looking like a Spanish fortress set to guard the pink-tinged sands, the grey rocks and the gold-reflected blue sea. But at first she had time for none of them. She saw very little even of Griselda during her first fortnight at Golden Grove, and it was only when she was in her third week on Dream Island that Griselda's listless air reproached her.

It was a brilliant morning. She had just seen Bill White off on his return home for convalescence and she had intended to spend the day looking up her mothers-to-be and reminding them that their clinic—or party as they preferred it to be called—was to be held the next day. But her first duty, she decided, was to Griselda.

She said, "Now Bill White has gone I can manage to take a day off, I think. I can leave word where I'm to be found if an emergency comes up. Shall we go down on the beach and have a lazy morning down there, dipping in and out of the sea? We might take lunch with us if you would like that."

Griselda looked at her with resentment.

"You haven't bothered to spend much time with me up to now," she remarked coldly.

"I've had to find my way about everything," Jan reminded her. "And Bill's accident made rather a rush. This is my first day free. So what shall we do? Would you rather go somewhere else?"

"Where else is there to go?" Griselda demanded. She looked at Jan between her lashes in a way her friend had learnt to distrust. "I don't think I'll bother to go anywhere," she decided.

"Yes, you will." Jan became firm. "I don't know what this semi-invalid act you put on here is all about, but it won't wash with me, you know. I saw you on board ship, remember."

Griselda's lips set sulkily; then she pulled herself out of her rocking-chair.

"Oh, come on, then," she remarked ungraciously. "But don't bring any food; it won't be needed."

Jan rather wondered exactly what was meant by that, but she did not bother to ask. She collected her swimsuit and together they made their way down the cliff to the beach.

Griselda did no more than her somewhat spectacular dangling of feet in the water and then her graceful posing of her body on the sand, a shady hat covering the back of her neck. But Jan was used to that, and after a time she swam out into the part netted off from the onslaught of sharks and barracudas.

It was very peaceful. Almost the only sound that came to her was the gentle lapping of the water. Even the noises from the shore were muted in this magical hour. She was glad enough to lie on her back, allowing the soft give-and-take waves to carry her backwards and forwards as gently as though she had been rocking in a cradle.

At last, she turned to swim back to the beach. Griselda was no longer alone. A man was seated on the sand by her side, talking to her with what seemed even from this distance to be a particular earnestness. Jan's heart gave a lurch of alarm when she saw that it was Luis, and then she told herself not to be a fool. Naturally, on this tiny island, Griselda could not avoid meeting him.

Nevertheless, she swam back to the beach and climbed up towards them, wrapping her towel round her shoulders and pulling off her cap to shake free her hair.

"Oh, Jan," Griselda called out to her as soon as she came near enough. "I'm going out with Luis. On his yacht, you know."

It was her guilty air that gave the show away. If it had not been for that, Jan might have thought that the invitation was a chance one, but Griselda could not keep back the half-defiant, half-triumphant sidelong glance of a child caught raiding the jam cupboard. Quite obviously the meeting had been pre-arranged. How many others had there been—as secret as this one was meant to be—while Leslie, Nicolas and Jan were all at work? Jan looked uncertainly from one to the other.

"Hello, Jan." Luis hailed her cheerfully and bestowed upon her an impenitent wink behind Griselda's back. "I'm glad to say I've managed to make life rather less boring for Griselda. She's becoming quite a sailswoman. What about you? Will you come with us today?"

Griselda stiffened; her lips set mutinously and her eyes theatened Jan. Quite obviously Jan would be an unwanted third on the yacht, but perhaps that would be all for the best. She might even be able to see Luis alone and tell him what she thought of his behaviour. Not that it was likely to have much effect, but it would give her some satisfaction. Her anger rose as she saw the look of smug triumph on his handsome face and turned to look at the transformed animation on Griselda's.

"I'll come," she decided, and had no idea that, by so promising, she would alter the course of the future.

CHAPTER EIGHT

LUIS LED THE WAY round the promontory towards his own private stretch of beach. His large, fortress-like house, square with a patio in the centre, its windows, slits in it dark frontage, sprawled across the edge of the cliff. Jan had never been here yet and was surprised to see the difference in so small a space of land. A short, squat breakwater jutted out into the sea, and a blue and white dinghy, tied to the end of it, rocked gently backwards and forwards on the swell. A short way out, a small but beautiful yacht, its sides white, blue-marked, its sails almost silver in the sun, lay motionless as a statue growing from the blue of the sea.

"Here we are," Luis announced. "You've deserted me completely, Jan—quite gone over to the enemy's camp—so I've never had a chance to show you this. Do you like sailing?"

"I haven't done much," Jan confessed, but her voice was drowned as Griselda cut in sharply with, "What do you mean by the enemy's camp?"

"Jan knows." Luis twinkled a message of understanding at her, cutting Griselda out of their private intimacy. Griselda gave Jan a look of sheer hatred. Jan stiffened; she knew quite well what Luis meant, but there was no need for him to turn it into a secret between them. She was so busy looking her resentment at him that she never noticed Griselda's gritted teeth and thinly tightened lips.

Luis, for his part, seemed totally unaware of any cross-currents flowing around him. He spoke easily to both of them as he led the way towards the dinghy. When they were settled in it, he rowed with swift, sure strokes to the yacht and helped them both aboard.

"Welcome to the *Water Lily*—my most treasured possession," he said, waving his hands round the white trimness of the little boat. She was small—only for local sailing—but perfect in every detail and glowing in the sunlight like some lovely, proud bird.

An old colored man who was busy at one end of the deck straightened himself up and came towards them.

"You not go sailing in the *Lily* today, sir?" he asked anxiously. "I don't like the weather."

"Nonsense!" Luis waved this away. "It's as calm as a looking-glass."

"Now it is," the man agreed. "But not soon. There's a tiny cloud 'way over on the horizon and a lull in the wind that means it may blow up into a storm soon. The rainy season's not quite at an end, sir. Nor the hurricane time, come to that. And the *Lily's* not too safe in a storm. Them sails that I told you about——"

"Oh, for Pete's sake, man, stop being such a dismal croaker!" Luis broke into his words. "There's no storm about and there's not going to be one!"

The man shook his head without speaking. Jan saw the anxious roll of his eyes and nervous pucker that drew his brows together; she was going to suggest that they postpone the trip when Luis turned to Griselda.

"What about it, Griselda?" he asked. "Do you want to put off our sail?"

Griselda looked up at him adoringly.

"Why should we?" she asked indifferently. "Some people believe in all sorts of omens that come to nothing."

"Oh, he's just a superstitious old man, afraid of his own shadow sometimes!" Luis ground out the words. Both of them had spoken as though the old sailor had not been there at all. Jan saw the quickly hidden look of embarrassment on his face and the patience in his eyes, and her anger rose.

Before she could speak, however, Luis turned to the man and said abruptly, "Very well, Joseph. You needn't come with us if you're scared. I can manage the *Water Lily* perfectly well by myself and I'd rather be without your moans if you're in that sort of mood. Get along ashore and find something to do there."

"Very well, sir." The man lowered himself into the dinghy, but Jan called out before he rowed away, "Wait a minute, Luis. After all he does know all about the coast and we don't. Why should he lie about the weather? Don't you think we ought to put it off?"

"Oh, Jan, don't interfere. Luis knows what he's doing," Griselda told her petulantly. "But if you're afraid, there's no need for you to come with us. We're going, aren't we, Luis?"

"Of course, my sweet. But, as you say, there's no need for Jan to come if she's afraid," Luis agreed, his eyes twinkling in sheer devilment at Jan, daring her to come.

Jan flushed and pushed back the angry words she wanted so badly to say.

"You know perfectly well that I shall come if you insist on going," she retorted, her head high. "You know you're an idiot, Griselda."

She knew the last words were a mistake, even before they were properly out, but she could no more restrain them than she could help breathing. Griselda's mouth shut like a trap.

"If you minded your own business, we would all get on a good deal better," she snapped.

Luis held up a restraining hand.

"Ladies! Ladies!" he besought them, laughing nevertheless. "All right, Joseph," he added to the old negro. "Cut along. Keep an eye open for our return and bring the dinghy out to meet us."

Joseph rowed away, his face worried, muttering under his breath. But Luis turned with another laugh.

"I'll get her started," he said. "And then we'll have some wine and biscuits. Don't look so glum, Jan. I haven't seen you for ages. Surely you're not going to spoil all my pleasure at seeing you again?"

"You know quite well why I came," Jan told him steadily, even though she knew he was quite impervious to hints and snubs. "I told you before——"

He grinned at her.

"That's what I like about you, Jan," he remarked. "You're so forthright. Never mind, my sweet; you liked me for myself once and you'll do it again before I've finished with you, I promise."

Griselda broke pettishly into the conversation.

"I wouldn't for the world interrupt your simple pleasures," she said with heavy sarcasm. "But I'm getting tired of sitting here with the sun baking my head. When are we going to make a start?"

"At once, Madam." Luis bowed to her and walked away. Griselda's face was dark with sullen anger as she turned a shoulder towards Jan, averting her face.

Jan did not in the least mind being cut by Griselda, but she was both annoyed and worried. Annoyed at the difficult position in which she found herself, worried not only by the threat of bad weather — which, after all, she supposed Luis could cope with — but, more still, by the sudden remembrance that she had not let anyone at Golden Grove know what she was going to do. If a bad case came in; if she was wanted in a hurry, what would they do? She thought of Bill White. If she had not been there then to help with the operation, his chances would have been much slighter. What if another accident case was brought in while she was out on the sea? She made a quick movement to ask Luis to put her ashore, even if it did mean leaving Griselda alone with him. But it was too late. She heard the purr of the auxiliary motor engine and realized that the shore was getting farther and farther away.

Luis came towards them, wiping his hands on a bit of cotton waste.

"Come on down to the cabin," he said. "I've set her course, so as long as I keep a general look-out, I needn't be at the wheel all the time. But I've got out some refreshments, so let's have them while we've got the chance."

"As long as you know what you're doing," Griselda objected, as she followed down to the tiny cabin. She did not look quite so assured or so certain that she wanted the trip now, and Jan guessed that she had had very strong second thoughts on the subject, though she did not intend to let anyone know.

The half-hour that passed while Luis entertained them in his cabin was one of the most uncomfortable Jan had ever known. Griselda made not the slightest effort to make herself agreeable or even polite, while Jan herself was too worried about the hospital to enjoy the excellent Spanish wine or rich cakes with which Luis plied them.

The yacht gave a sudden lurch and he broke off in the middle of a sentence.

"It's all right," he assured them. "But I'll just go and see that everything's under control."

They followed him on deck and Jan, standing by Griselda, heard her catch her breath in sudden alarm.

The small grey cloud which had sat so quietly on the horizon had spread till the whole sky was grey. The wind was rising; even as they reached the open, it swooped down with alarming suddenness upon them, ripping apart the clouds in its wild descent and sending them scurrying hither and thither like a terrified flock of wild birds.

The *Water Lily* lurched from one side to the other, dipping so low that she almost shipped water. The sails started to flap in the storm, their white purity smirched by dashing spray and blackened waves. Luis made a rush to furl them, but even as he did so there was a reverberating crash of thunder, the whole sky was torn apart by a jagged zigzag of lightning and then a sheet of rain came down upon them. It did not fall, Jan thought, struggling for breath, clutching at the rail to keep herself from being dashed overboard; there seemed simply to be a hole torn in the sky and a deluge fell through it. Blinding, choking, impenetrable. In a couple of seconds they were wet through, their clothes clinging to them, their hair lank in their eyes, their faces stinging with the force of it.

Luis was caught by the fury and thrown against the rails. The sails bent beneath the onslaught; there was a cracking sound and slowly, grindingly, one of the masts began to fall.

"Look out!" he screamed at them. "Get below!"

The wind tore the words from his mouth and scattered them into the roaring gale. Only the movement of his lips showed them that he was talking and gave them any idea of his meaning. But Griselda, in any case, was beyond taking any orders, beyond doing anything to help herself. Buffeted by the wind, clothes clinging limply to her, streams of water pouring down her face and tangling the rich beauty of her hair into lank, colourless rat's tails, she threw her arms round Luis' neck as he pulled himself to his feet and clung to him with all the strength of desperation.

"You sent the dinghy away!" she moaned. "We'll be washed overboard! We'll be drowned! And the sharks — they'll get us!"

Her voice rose into a scream of terror. Luis pulled her hands roughly away from him, almost overbalancing her.

"Stop it!" he shouted. "If you get hysterical, I shall slap you hard. There's no point in screeching about what may happen. We've got to see that it doesn't! For goodness' sake, leave me alone and let me do something to save the yacht! Jan, take her away and knock some sense into her. And keep out of my way, both of you. You can't do any good and you can do a lot of harm."

Jan could not hear his words, but as he thrust Griselda at her, she gathered the general import and, putting her arm round the hysterical girl, she pulled her out of the way while Luis worked frantically to save the masts and sails.

The *Water Lily* listed heavily over to one side. Waves dashed over the deck; Jan thought she saw the black sharpness of a fin and then told herself firmly that she was imagining things. She could keep her head and do all she could to help if there was a likelihood only of drowning, but if there were sharks—She shuddered and turned her attention to Griselda, who was struggling in her arms.

There was only one thing to be done and Jan did it. Her hand shot out and she slapped Griselda sharply in the face. Griselda moved back, putting her hand to her cheek, her eyes glaring hate at Jan, but the blow sobered her and she stopped screaming.

Suddenly her eyes became fixed and glazed. She seemed to forget her anger with Jan as she caught hold of her arm, shouting, "Look!" above the clamour of the wind.

Jan steadied herself and followed the direction of her pointing finger. There was a tiny black spot in the distance, tossing up and down on the waves, almost covered by spray and deluged by rain, but coming slowly nearer.

"The dinghy!" Griselda gasped. "They're coming towards us! They've come to rescue us! But will they ever make it?"

CHAPTER NINE

LATER, THEIR RESCUE from the submerging yacht seemed to Jan like a nightmare. The sort where all details are blurred, leaving a general impression of horror and fear without any clear memory of individual happenings. Somehow the dinghy reached them; somehow the now fainting Griselda was helped on board, somehow Luis, grim-faced and light-lipped, was persuaded to leave his once beautiful plaything and return with them. They made the return journey safely; Joseph, Luis and Nicolas — whose presence Jan did not at the time even feel surprised about — took the oars in turn, while the two girls gasped and shivered, thrown from this side to that, the little boat tossing about, one moment on top of the waves, the next almost submerged. Jan felt too sick and ill to know what was happening, but she managed to keep her wits about her enough to look after Griselda, whose condition was piteous.

Time lost all meaning and she had no idea how long it took them to reach the shore or crawl, limp, bedraggled and wretched, towards Luis' house.

"It is nearest," he explained. "You must all come in to dry and recover from the strain. I only wish your first visit could have been made under happier circumstances, Jan, but you will forgive me, I hope."

He seemed to have recovered his spirits again and he picked Griselda up in his arms and carried her towards the grey house on the cliff.

Nicolas took Jan's arm and followed, bending against the wind and pausing for a moment as another great flash of lightning ripped open the sky. Reaction had set in and her legs were trembling so much now that she would have been glad of more support, but a glance at his face stopped her from speaking. She had never seen it so dark or so angry; the tight line of his lips and the heavy drawing of his brows made him look dangerous, and the small shiver she gave was not entirely due to the cold.

As soon as they were inside the house, the housekeeper took charge of them, drew hot baths for them, helped them to change into clothes provided by the various maids and brushed their hair — particularly Griselda's glorious locks, which at once recovered their spring and brilliance — till they felt better able to face the others.

Griselda seemed, in fact, to have recovered with surprising ease. She had, Jan considered, the resilience of a child —the same capacity for tears and laughter, the same quick recovery after complete collapse. But she did not speak a word to Jan while they were changing, and every now and again threw glances of resentment and dislike at her.

Luis and Nicolas were in the study — a large, high-ceilinged room with long windows overlooking the central patio and old-fashioned Spanish garden. Luis now seemed to have recovered his temper and spirits, and poured out glasses of wine with a smile at his guests. Jan scarcely looked at him, however; her gaze was fixed on Nicolas, whose face was as stern as it had been on their climb up to the house.

"I want to get things straightened out," he said, as soon as Luis had settled them all comfortably in easy chairs. "Sorry, Luis, to drag you into this, but I've got to find out what it's all about."

"Really, old man. The girls must be exhausted," Luis protested, but Nicolas took no notice.

"An emergency case was brought in," he said. "I sent for you, Jan, but you were nowhere to be found. Surely you know that you ought to leave word where you're going if you decide to take time off? It would be more considerate to ask me first, but I'll let that pass. Did you really go out on that yacht without leaving word? Or is there some excuse I know nothing about?"

Jan felt the colour flood her cheeks.

"No; there's no excuse," she told him steadily. "I decided to go on the spur of the moment and I forgot to leave a message."

She thought that, for a moment, Nicolas' face changed, that there was a look of hurt disappointment upon it, but then his lips tightened and his voice was hard as he went on.

"Joseph came to me because he was worried. He said that he had warned you all of the coming storm, but one of the young ladies had insisted upon going. One had not wanted to go, but had been over-persuaded. I suppose——"

Griselda broke into his words.

"I didn't want to go!" she cried, her voice rising on a note of hysteria. "I begged Jan to stay, but she would go and she wanted me to go, too. Because she likes everything to be correct and her barrister fiancé mightn't like her going off alone with Luis; though it's rather late in the day to think of that now. After the way she went on —— And it was horrible! ..I feel so ill!"

Her voice became a wail. Nicolas' eyes flicked over her, professionally seeking what damage had been done. But this was too much for Jan. She was willing to shield Griselda from her foolishness, but not to this extent. Spite had got the better of all Griselda's other feelings, she knew, but there was a limit to what Jan could stand.

"That's all wrong!" she protested. "You know it was the other way round! Wasn't it, Luis?"

Luis eyes met her, and an imp of devilry danced in them. She knew, even before he spoke, that he would find it amusing to pay her back for her outspokenness by making her seem in the wrong, so her feeling of bitter anger and helpless injustice was unmixed with surprise when he shook his head sadly.

"Sorry, Jan my dear. I would do a lot for you," he said. "But we must not allow others to suffer for our misdoings. No, we are to blame — you and I. I because I was so anxious to go out with you, whatever the cost. You because you persuaded Griselda against her better judgment."

The feeling that welled up in Jan was a sort of helplessness. She knew, without looking, just what the expression on Nicolas' face must be. There was only one possible construction he could put on things, and how could she blame him? He must imagine that she was so man-mad that she had rushed after Luis as soon as he beckoned to her, losing her head so completely that she forgot all about the hospital and her duty there and dragged Griselda into possible danger against her will. As if that was not bad enough, he must believe that she had deliberately lied to save herself, and if he thought he could not believe her in that one thing, why should he expect to believe her in any other? He must have lost trust in her completely. It would spoil all their future relationship and her work at the hospital. At that moment she hated Luis, and when she turned upon him her eyes were blazing.

"I don't know what your idea is," she said softly. "Or, at least, I think I know only too well. But you've done the meanest thing you possibly could and I don't believe I can ever forgive you!"

She did not know whether Nicolas could hear her or not. Possibly not, she thought, for he had turned away from her in what she supposed was disgust and was watching Griselda, who now caused a diversion.

"I do feel ill!" she wailed. "You know I'm not strong. You know I can't stand all this sort of thing. And it was terrible! Please, Nick, take me home!"

Nicolas took a quick step towards her.

"Yes, dear," he promised her. "The rain has stopped for the time being. I'll take you straight back and Jan shall get you off to bed."

Griselda certainly did look ill, her face white, great shadows darkening her eyes, her hands trembling. Some of it was caused by shock, but Jan could not help wondering whether part was simply fear of being found out. However, everyone had forgotten Jan now. Luis said quickly, "I'll get my car and run you round. Mrs. Duncarron can't walk," and then, bowing over Griselda's hand, added softly, "How can you ever forgive me, my dear?"

Griselda pulled her hand away, her lips quivering as though she were trying not to cry. Jan smothered her anger and tucked a soft Spanish shawl round her patient to stop her shivering. Then they all went out to the car, standing sleek and expensive in the courtyard where rivulets of water still ran over the cobbled stones.

"Shall I sit with Griselda?" Jan asked, but Nicolas replied sharply, "No. You'd better sit in front with Luis. I'll look after Griselda."

As though she were not to be trusted, thought Jan bitterly. But she climbed silently into the front of the car and waited while Nicolas put his arm round Griselda, holding her gently to avoid jolting.

"How could you?" Jan asked Luis bitterly when they had started. "You've spoilt my job for me completely."

He twinkled down at her, quite unrepentant.

"You really did deserve a little punishment, didn't you?" he asked. "It was more than I could resist. Besides, my dear, if someone has to be angry with me, I would rather it was you than Griselda. But you need not worry, I am sure. The good Nicolas will learn your worth too thoroughly to think again of this little mishap."

"Little mishap?" Amazement took away Jan's voice. "When—when——"

"Yes, my dear. When you were both nearly drowned and when I lost my beloved *Water Lily.*" His voice became serious. "And poor Griselda looking so ill. I should be ashamed of myself, I know, but I find it difficult to be serious, even with myself."

Jan pursed her lips, well aware that it was quite useless to pursue the subject. But she knew that the matter was far from finished, as far as she was concerned; in fact, she had an uncomfortable feeling that it had only just begun.

Griselda's temperature was high by the time they reached Golden Grove. In spite of the clammy heat, she was shivering uncontrollably, even after Jan had filled a hot-water bottle and settled her in bed with a hot drink. Nicolas gave her an injection and they waited till she had fallen asleep.

"The emergency!" Jan exclaimed as they left the room. "I'd forgotten."

"There's no need to worry," Nicolas assured her coldly. "I managed with Sarah-Ann's help. She was wonderful. And there seems no point in going on with this. Forget the whole matter, for goodness' sake."

Forget? But she knew that could never be quite true. However much he meant to, he would always find himself thinking of it when a sudden emergency arose or when she had to take unexpected responsibility. He would remember that time when she had failed him and would wonder whether it was safe to leave everything to her now. And there was nothing—nothing at all—she could do to make him realize the truth. He would always go on thinking these things of her.

She had been so proud of the trust he reposed in her, so pleased with the progress she was making in the island, that tears smarted at the back of her eyes. She shook her head a little to push them back; she could not bear him to see them.

But there seemed little chance of that. He was staring thoughtfully at Griselda's door and, when he spoke, it was to say, "I don't like the look of her, you know. I know she's neurotic, but that makes her all the more susceptible to shock. And the shock she has had, added to the wetting and physical strain, have pulled her down pretty thoroughly. I don't want her in a raging fever."

Jan found that her voice was almost timid as she answered, "I'll stay with her all the time."

He shook his head.

"No; better not," he told her. "You'll only remind her of what happened. I'll take over here. You go along to the hospital and look after our case there. I've got him under observation. May have to operate tomorrow, but I may be able to treat him without. Sarah-Ann's in charge at present, but it's too much for her, really, though she has been absolutely wonderful. I didn't know she had it in her."

His voice was warm with affectionate admiration. Jan did not know why she winced away from the sound of it; perhaps because she was so tired and her head ached so badly and people seemed to approve of or be sorry for everyone but her. She would have given anything in the world, at that moment, for someone—anyone at all—to have said, "You poor darling, Jan! You did all you could for Griselda. How are you feeling now? Don't you think you ought to lie down and rest?"

That was only self-pity, though, and she hated that. She must forget how tired she was and how bitterly the feeling of injustice rankled in her.

She managed to pull herself together, but not before Nicolas glanced at her and asked, "Do you feel well enough? After all, you went through this too."

Perhaps she imagined that he added silently to himself, "Although you brought it all on." That wouldn't do, she told herself; if she went on thinking people were blaming her when they didn't actually say so, she would end up with a persecution complex. She managed to smile at this idea and to answer briskly, "I'm quite well enough," although she felt nothing of the sort. Her legs were absurdly weak and wobbly, her head was swimming and her hands trembling, but she did not mean to let anyone know this. At least, they shouldn't have any justifiable cause for complaint.

But, for the first time since he had rescued them, Nicolas looked at her approvingly and spoke with his old warmth. "Good girl!" he said. "Off with you, then! Send Sarah-Ann home. And if there's any change in Mortimer, let me know at once."

Jan stopped only to put on her uniform, and then she hurried across to the hospital where the new patient, a very ancient negro who rejoiced in the name of Mortimer Clarence, was drowsing uneasily.

Sarah-Ann was sitting by his bed. She jumped to her feet when Jan came in, but the look of almost ludicrous disappointment on her face when she saw her showed that she had been hoping to see Nicolas.

"I've come to take over," Jan told her. "Nicolas said you were to go home. And," she added, seeing the look of disappointment on the girls face, "he asked me to thank you for the wonderful way you coped. He can't come himself because Griselda's ill. I'm going to make myself a cup of coffee while Mortimer's asleep. Would you like one before you go home?"

Sarah-Ann agreed without much enthusiasm, and followed Jan to the small kitchen in the rear of the building. She watched while Jan put the coffee on to boil, and then she suddenly burst out with, "I wish you hadn't come! Things are so different now! The only times I see Nick alone are the times when he's so busy over his hospital that he can't be bothered to think about me!"

"But he did think about you today—quite a lot," Jan told her gently. She felt immeasurably older than this child, although in years there was not a great deal of difference. But Sarah-Ann had never had to do anything for herself, never even had to think for herself. She had been given everything she wanted all her life, and when, for the first time, it seemed as though she could not easily have the one thing she had set her heart upon, she was puzzled and hurt and resentful. "He told me you were wonderful and he didn't think you had it in you. And it isn't I who have taken him from you; it's just that he's a wonderful doctor and his work is his vocation. I think it will always come first with him."

"Will it?" Sarah-Ann sighed. She sat hugging her knees, her head thrown back and one silvery-gold lock of hair falling over her forehead in a youthful, appealing way. Her face looked lost and earnest, and when she turned to Jan it wore a friendly expression towards her for almost the first time.

"I'll try not to be jealous," she asserted. "I know the hospital means such a terrible lot to him and that you're part of it. The trouble is that when you're so frightfully in love with a person, you want to share everything and to have absolutely every bit of him. At least, I do. But I really do want to share his interests and let him know I'm not a grabbing sort and do understand. That's why I wanted to help him here. So that I could get to know all about the life that's his here and that I didn't share at all. But—but it doesn't seem to bring us any nearer. And I do love him so terribly much that it hurts!"

Jan did not quite know what to say and Sarah-Ann continued, "Before he opened the hospital, we used to ride together every day and I thought he loved me. And now I don't know. It's awful not knowing——"

She broke off suddenly, reddening a little, the colour creeping up under the soft fairness of her skin as she turned to look at Jan warily from the corner of her eyes.

"For Pete's sake—how I've been running on!" she exclaimed, with a would-be return to lightness. "You must think me an utter chump! You know what? I hated you when you first came, but I don't any more. I rather like you."

She slid off the table and said shamefacedly, "Forget all this, won't you? And I don't think I'd better wait for the coffee. Dad worries when I'm too late getting home—goodness knows why!—and he'll be wondering where I've got to."

And, with a jaunty bob of her pony-tail, she ran to the door, and Jan heard her footsteps retreat down the corridor before she turned to pour herself out a much-needed cup of coffee.

CHAPTER TEN

JAN ARRANGED THE light so that it did not shine on Mortimer Clarence's face, and after making sure that there was nothing more she could do for him she retired to the table at the other end of the room and took out her writing-pad.

So many things had happened during the day that she was terribly afraid of falling asleep just when she was wanted, in spite of the many cups of black coffee she had taken. It was the most depressing part of the night, when tiny things assume giant proportions and the darkness outside seems to seep hopelessly into the heart — when things appear ten times worse than they do in the daytime and it seems impossible to have enough strength to face up to them.

It was very quiet in the hospital. Already Jan was becoming so used to the constant soundfulness of the tropics that she scarcely noticed the ceaseless whirr of the crickets, the croak of a bull-frog, the defiant crowing of a cock, reversing all the laws of nature by boldly asserting that it was already time for him to be stirring, the distant braying of a wakeful donkey. So the night seemed still. The rain had ended after the earlier downfall; the thunder died away; the wind subsided as though it had never been. In spite of all her years of nursing, Jan had always hated these eerie hours in the night and now, quite alone in the building but for the heavily breathing Mortimer, she found herself shivering with dread.

She had, she thought wearily, quite a lot to dread. Griselda was in the throes of fever, her temperature soaring in spite of all Nicolas had done to bring it down. This time, there was no imagination in her illnes. What was more, she had evidently poured out her version of the day's happenings to Leslie; what that had been, Jan could only surmise, but the result had been enough to make him glance at Jan with an expression of sheer dislike and distrust, and almost to shudder away from her.

With all her heart Jan longed suddenly to be away from here. To be back in England, with her mother who would make things seem right by the very force of her affection, with her father whose clear common sense would help. Above all, with Roderick. She longed, more than she had ever done, to have him with her now. To feel the strength of his arms round her, to see his eyes twinkling down at her with the love and admiration in them clear for her to see, to hear his voice as he told her that he loved her.

She choked back a sigh and, picking up her pad, started to write to him, pouring out all her longing.

"I'll be home in the spring," she promised him. "Once the hospital is on its feet, I won't feel mean about leaving. And it isn't very long till then, as long as I know you love me. But I miss you so tonight that I feel as if I just can't go on without you."

Mortimer stirred in his sleep and called out something. She went across to him, putting her pad down on the table. When she had attended to him, it was time to wash him, make his bed and bring him the breakfast Lily had come across to cook for him, so the letter had to be pushed away to be finished later.

Nicolas was the next arrival at the hospital. He looked brisk and business-like, and as far as his manner towards Jan was concerned the day before might never have been.

"I think we can clear this up without an operation," he announced with satisfaction. "I'll stay with him now. Sarah-Ann is coming along to help. You run along and have breakfast and then go to bed. You look done in."

Jan felt absurdly touched by his concern. She said, with a gulp, because talking about it made her remember yesterday too vividly, "How's Griselda?"

"Not too good." He looked worried. "She goes down so suddenly. Doesn't seem to have the will-power to fight anything, and, of course, she's always sure she's dying, which doesn't help. But unless anything unforeseen happens, we'll pull her through. I suppose I ought to go and look up Luis to see how he is. After all, he went through quite a lot yesterday, even if he did allow you to talk him into doing something he must have known was sheer madness."

"But I didn't——" Jan was beginning, but she stopped there and clamped her lips tightly together. Why should he believe her now if he had not done so yesterday? He would only think she was lying senselessly.

He looked at her curiously when she started to talk, and as she broke off he touched her arm gently.

"Dont worry," he said softly. "Everyone does some idiotic thing on the spur of the moment and regrets it bitterly afterwards. It isn't as terrible as all that."

She did not answer, because he had no idea that the most terrible part of all was the injustice of it. He went on, "Run off now and don't get up till you feel thoroughly rested. You've been rather wonderful, carrying on like this."

And as she turned towards the door, more touched by his praise than she had been by any blame, he called out after her, "The ship called in early this morning, so the mail will be along soon. Something to look forward to."

Indeed it was, she thought. A letter from Roderick; perhaps several letters. She walked with renewed vigour across to the house, where Leslie was sitting on the verandah having his breakfast.

He pulled her chair out for her and then returned glumly to his.

"Griselda wants to see you," he shot suddenly out at her. "I don't know why. But for goodness' sake, don't upset her."

"I am a nurse and I do know better than that," she could not resist reminding him.

He had the grace to color, but he did not speak to her again, and as soon as he had hurried over his coffee, he got up and left.

Jan dragged herself to her feet. It was an effort, for her wakeful night on top of the day of strain had now caught up with her. All she longed for was to drag off her clothes and feel the sting of cold water on her in a shower-bath and then throw herself down on her bed to sleep. For hours, she felt now. But if Griselda wanted her, she must see what was wrong. In her feverish state she must be kept quiet, and Jan's rigorous training helped her to repress her own feelings for the good of her patient.

Griselda, hot and flushed with fever, greeted her excitedly.

"I'm going to die, Jan," she announced. "I know I'm going to die and I feel so terribly ashamed of myself!"

"Of course you're not going to die," Jan contradicted her. "Don't let me hear any more nonsense like that. You're feverish from shock and chill, but the sooner you calm down and realize you've got to help yourself to get better, the sooner it will happen."

"You've always got so much common sense, Jan," Griselda told her, lying back on her pillows with a sigh of relief. "I feel different when I'm with you. As if things were simple. And when you've gone, they get complicated again. But I'm sorry, Jan. For the lie I told. I didn't mean to get you into trouble. At least, yes, I did a little," she confessed. "I'd been so cross with you for coming too and spoiling everything and for making Luis be nice to you. He likes you, you know; he told me so one day. He said he was more than half in love with you. He felt differently about you from any other girl. He said that if only you would be serious about him, he would be tempted to turn over a new leaf and marry you. And that makes me horribly jealous, because he wouldn't marry me. Even if he does like making love to me more than to you," she could not help adding complacently.

Jan sat down on the end of the bed.

"You're talking complete nonsense," she said. "And please get this straight in your head. I'm taking all this trouble for Leslie's sake. Because he's too nice to be hurt and you are the only thing that matters to him. But I am very cross with you—and with Luis too—for getting me into this position. It has spoilt everything for me at the hospital. Nicolas thinks I'm not to be trusted any more and it has made things terribly difficult."

"I know. And I'm most awfully sorry," Griselda declared, the corners of her lips turning down as though she meant to cry. "I'll make up to you for it. I promise you I will. As soon as I'm well, I'll show everyone how much I like you and trust you. Only don't tell about yesterday.

Please don't! It would hurt Leslie so terribly. I just couldn't bear it!"

Jan longed to tell her that if she learnt to bear a bit more, it would be much better both for her and her husband, but, remembering in time their nurse-patient status, she contented herself with saying, "I won't say anything. And now, settle down to rest. There's nothing at all to get excited about. I shall expect to see you quite well again by tomorrow."

But once she stepped outside the door, exhaustion clamped itself down upon her again with renewed force. She did not know how she would manage to crawl as far as her room or pull her clothes off before she fell asleep. But as she crossed the hall she met Lily, carrying a collection of letters.

"The mail from England," the girl announced cheerfully. "Lots for you, Miss Jan. They'll make you happy."

"I'm sure they will," Jan agreed, taking the letters Lily held out to her and going on her way to her room, feeling already less tired. Two from her mother, one from her father, a couple from nurse friends from the hospital at home and three from Roderick. Two sent by ordinary mail and one air mail.

She sat down on her bed, sorting them out and holding those from Roderick tightly in her hand. She would sleep all the better if she had renewed assurance of Rodericks love.

The first was written just after seeing her off on the ship and was as full of love and longing as even she could desire. The second, written a week later, was hurried. He had been busy—a brief that might make all the difference to his professional career. He was taking out the daughter of the famous barrister, Sir Haleby Moore, that evening. He was sure Jan was far too sensible to mind. It would make all the difference if Sir Haleby was willing to put some briefs in his way.

Jan was far from sensible where love was concerned and she found that she did mind, intensely. However, she tore open the last letter, hoping that she would find consolation in that.

"I have thought and thought," he wrote. "And it isn't fair to you to expect you to be tied to me for so long. For I just can't afford to be married for ages. Besides, there is the question of your health. It looks as though you may have to live abroad for a couple of years or so. I couldn't be selfish enough to ask you to come home and face the damp here if it would harm you."

Jan looked at the date with a puzzled frown. It was written only a few days ago and sent by air mail as far as that would go. A fortnight after the last somewhat unsatisfactory one. She saw the hand of his mother in the remarks about her health; Mrs. Dentram had made continual digs about that and had purposely appeared to misunderstand Jan when she had explained that there was nothing actually wrong with her. But Roderick had known that this winter abroad had been only a precautionary measure. Why was he writing like this? She continued reading.

"So it wouldn't be much of a life for you, living in the West Indies and engaged to a man at home you can't ever see. I hate to hurt you, Jan, and you must know that there will never be anyone quite like you. I shall always remember you, but the whole thing is so impossible that, for your own sake, we ought to break it off, so that you can make yourself forget me as soon as possible."

Jan's hands felt limp and the letter fluttered out of them. He was breaking it off. However he might try to wrap it up, out of regard for her feelings—or his own!—he did not want to marry her. Her engagement—all her life at home that had been bound up in him, consisting only of her love for him, her hopes for the future—everything was over. Finished as surely as if it had never been.

CHAPTER ELEVEN

SLEEP SEEMED TO have left Jan entirely now. Although she went automatically through the motions of undressing, bathing and getting into bed, she soon found that there was no chance of rest. Roderick's words ran through and through her mind. She thought now, looking back, that she must have known at the back of her mind all the time that he would discover that she was not the right wife for him.

He had been in love with her. Deeply and honestly in love; she did him the justice to believe that. But he was ambitious; she remembered the hundreds of times he had talked to her about the great things he meant to do, the heights to which he intended to climb. If she had stayed in England, his love might have been strong enough to overlook everything else. But, with so great a distance between them, with his mother continually pointing out to him Jan's unimportance, her ill health—for nothing would convince the good lady that there was nothing really wrong with her—the importance of marrying the right sort of wife—one who would further his career and not be a drain on it—Jan could bring herself to understand the uncertainty that had been born in him. If he hadn't met Diana Moore, if he had not seen how greatly her father could help him——But he had, and there was no use wondering what would have happened if things had turned out differently.

Because he might try to wrap things up, he might do all he could to spare Jan's feelings, but the fact remained that, whether or not he still loved her, ambition was stronger than love. He would marry Diana, Jan felt convinced of that. He would become famous and, probably, he would never even remember that once he had been on the point of making a fool of himself by marrying the daughter of an unimportant country doctor.

She remembered the letter she had written him during the night. The letter in which she had poured out all her love and her longing. Thank goodness she had never posted it! That would have been the last humiliation! For, beyond the bitter hurt of her love, the memory of all their happy times together, the dreams they had woven round their future, lay a deep, burning humiliation. She wasn't good enough for him. Wrap it up whatever way you liked, that was what it meant. And, still, she wanted him; she wanted him so terribly. Lying on her bed, heat pouring down on her from the still morning air, she knew that he was still deep in her heart, and she felt utterly friendless and alone. Nicolas and Leslie had completely revised their first good impression of her; Griselda was jealous and childlishly spiteful; Sarah-Ann too full of her love for Nicolas to think of anyone else. There was no one at all to whom Jan could turn for comfort.

Her lips tightened suddenly. There was her work. It sounded trite and poor consolation enough. The warmth and beauty of love and trust between man and woman was something very different from the hard toil of bringing health and hygiene to this tiny island. But it had been done before; people had thrown themselves wholeheartedly into their vocation and, in it, found complete content. Why should she not do the same? When memories of Roderick, of the way his eyes twinkled, of the deep timbre of his voice and the charm of his smile returned to start the nagging ache in her heart again, she tried to push them back. It would hurt for a long time, she knew, but she insisted upon remembering all the people who had got over unhappy love affairs and telling herself with a common sense she did not really feel that she would do the same.

As a beginning, she remembered suddenly that today was the clinic for the mothers-to-be on the island. They would expect to see her there and she would not disappoint them. Sleep was, in any case, impossible, so she would start to put all her good resolutions into effect at once. And she wouldn't think—she wouldn't! She would work herself till she was too tired for any coherent thought about anything but her work!

Methodically, she dressed in clean uniform, brushing her hair and arranging it under her cap with special care: glancing at herself in the mirror and taking great pains over her make-up to hide the dark shadows under her eyes and the unusual pallor of her cheeks. No one must know. She could not bear anyone to guess her secret.

She was successful. When she was ready, she looked smart and competent and self-assured, and no one could possibly have guessed that her heart was aching so that it took all her self-control not to break down.

Nicolas looked surprised to see her.

"You needn't come yet," he remarked. "I can take the clinic on my own today. You can't have had more than a couple of hours' rest."

"It's all I want," she assured him. "I feel fine."

"You look it," he answered promptly. "But, in my experience, when a girl who normally wears very little make-up plasters her face with the stuff, it usually means that there's something she wants to hide. Not," he told her thoughtfully, "that I've had a great deal of experience, but I still believe in the idea."

He paused a moment as though giving her the chance to tell him what was wrong, but she did not take advantage of it. If only yesterday had never happened, if he was still the considerate and friendly colleague, she might have told him everything, but he no longer trusted her; in spite of his courteous manners, there was a difference, more felt than seen or heard. Something had changed between them; something had gone wrong. And before she could decide whether to tell him any more, the door banged open and Sarah-Ann danced in.

"Hello, Jan; I thought you wouldn't be in," she called out. "My! Aren't you conscientious! Up with a patient all night and back here this afternoon for the clinic. I've brought a lot of cakes, Nick. I got Polly to make them for us. I thought we could make a real party of it and make all the women want to have babies just so that they could come to the clinic!"

Her manner was much more friendly towards Jan than it had ever been before, and she beamed happily at Nicolas.

"Hi! young lady, the birth-rate is quite high enough on the island as it is. You can't go bribing them to increase it," Nicolas laughed at her, pulling her pony-tail teasingly. "But it's good of you, Sarah-Ann; really good to think of it. It had quite slipped my memory."

"You see how competent and thoughtful I'm getting," she flashed back. "And, in return, suppose you think of me as a human being again for a change. I've just been a piece of furniture or something to you lately."

"A very decorative and charming piece of furniture, then," he assured her. "What's wrong? In what way have I failed?"

She put her head on one side, considering him through half-closed lids in a way which had probably been borrowed from one of her favourite film stars, Jan decided.

"Garth Owen wants me to go out with him," she announced with somewhat overdone indifference. "He's very nice. Not exactly romantic, but solid. I don't know that I'm exactly wild about him, but if I'm driven into his arms by other people's indifference—Do you know, Nick, you haven't asked me to go anywhere with you since you opened the hospital? And we were going bathing by moonlight, too! Remember?"

He laughed.

"Very well, infant," he agreed. "Tomorrow night suit you? And shall I ask Garth to come along too?"

She pulled a face at him.

"If you do, I shall monopolize him all evening and leave you completely alone!" she threatened. "Unless"—and her eyes slid sideways to Jan — "you ask Jan too as his partner."

"I don't know what Jan would have to say to that," Nicolas retorted.

Their banter tugged at Jan's heart. There seemed such a happy intimacy between them that she could not help thinking of herself and Roderick. But, luckily for her, she heard the first of the arrivals for the clinic coming in and called out, "Here they are! I do hope it will be a success."

She need not have worried about that. It was—almost literally—a roaring success. After Nicolas had examined the women and given them a little talk on elementary hygiene, in which most of them were lamentably lacking, the cakes were produced; Lily brought iced lemonade from the house and the party began. Soon someone started to sing; others took it up, and before long all the lovely, velvety voices were raised in old folk-songs and plaintive lullabies. When it was time to go, the women left reluctantly.

"Mamie Palmer'll be green with jealousy 'cause she ain't going to have a baby and can't come to the parties," one of them remarked when she said goodbye, causing Sarah-Ann to look meaningly at Nicolas and whisper, "There, what did I tell you?"

"As long as it helps them to take reasonable care of themselves and the babies," Nicolas answered, as the last one left. "It mightn't be a bad idea to have another do for young wives; teach them hygiene and so on and give them some idea of balanced diets instead of eternal beans and bananas."

"Who are you going to get to teach them?" Sarah-Ann asked. "I don't know if Jan adds cooking and dietary to her accomplishments, but I don't. And if she does much more, she'll be running the whole island."

Nicolas looked at Jan in quick repentance, but before he could apologize for the idea or she could assure him that she would be really pleased to try to meet the young girls on a common ground, Sarah-Ann tucked her hand into his arm and said, "Dad says he's got a book he promised to lend you, but he never sees you now to give it to you. Come back with me now."

"I ought to see Griselda," Nicolas objected. "And you ought to stop and help Jan to clear up here."

Nevertheless, when Jan assured him that she was quite happy to do the clearing up herself, he allowed himself to be persuaded to walk back with Sarah-Ann.

Jan was glad to hear them go. It had been a strain, pretending that nothing was the matter, and now she could, for a time, remove the "face" she had too carefully cultivated for their benefit. Her mouth drooped as she cleared plates and glasses, and her eyes held all the feeling she had restrained before.

She thought she was alone. Being alone, she decided, could be the most precious gift of all. A life containing no privacy, one entirely lived in company, must be the greatest strain and punishment there could be, her thoughts ran on. So she started so much that she dropped a tumbler to the floor when she heard a voice in the doorway.

"Jan—oh, you poor child; did I scare you?" Luis asked, standing in the open doorway, watching her as, with trembling hands, she picked up the bits and pieces. "I couldn't stay away. My conscience has been pricking me and I was worried about how you were after yesterday."

"There's nothing wrong with me," Jan answered, trying to speak with dignity. But this last intrusion when she had just allowed herself to be natural was too much for her. Tears pricked her eyes and, although she shook her head impatiently, she could not hide them altogether.

"But—oh, darling, what have I done?" Luis took a step towards her, removing the glass from her hand and bringing out his clean silk handkerchief. "Are you crying because of yesterday? Did they give you a bad time of it? My dear, I am sorry that I behaved so badly, but you'd made me angry and I wanted to lash out at you. But now I am not angry any more. I'll go and see the good Nicolas and tell him what really happened."

"No, you won't!" She took hold of his sleeve and gave it a little shake to emphasize her words. "Not now — while Griselda's so ill. I promised I wouldn't. And, anyway, that wasn't what was upsetting me. I'm—tired, I suppose."

"Look at me, Jan." Luis' voice was more gentle than she had ever heard it before and he put his hands on her shoulders to turn her towards him. "You're lying, you know. You're such a wretched little liar that anyone can tell. You may be tired—you must be, I expect—but that isn't what upset you."

She swallowed, trying to think of some excuse, and as she was doing so he bent his head and kissed her very gently on the forehead.

"Not even the fiancé in England could object to that, I think!" he said, his voice a trifle rueful.

"There isn't a fiancé in England. Not any more." Jan had not meant to tell him. The words seemed to be drawn out of her by his unexpected gentleness and concern. He was the only person who had cared, and the fact that he could play so mean a trick on her as he had done yesterday was forgotten in the sympathy of his words now. So her answer slipped out without her really realizing that it was coming.

"Darling!" His arms tightened round her. "He's broken it off? And you've just gone on as though nothing had happened? You poor little scrap! A dear, brave, idiotic little scrap! The man deserves to be shot!"

Consolation and sympathy had certainly come from the very last quarter in which she had expected it. But she did not think of that now; she only knew she was heart-sick and utterly weary and that he was kind.

"He oughtn't to be," she tried to protest. "I know I'm not the right sort of wife for him. He needs someone with money or influence to help him in his profession—someone important."

"Someone important!" Luis grated out the words till they sounded beneath contempt. "When you——Oh, well, I shan't say any more about him. I'm glad it's happened. That may sound a cruel thing to say, but the fellow obviously wasn't nearly good enough for you, and it leaves me a clear field."

She tried to pull herself away from him.

"Don't Luis—not now!" she protested. "I know you don't mean what you say, but——"

"But I do now," he broke in. "I can't explain it, but for the first time in my life I've met the one woman I want to marry. Indifference, perhaps. Opposition. I'm not used to it. It may have started out like that, but now it's real and true. I want to have you with me for always; I don't want anyone else now—the thought just makes me sick. Darling, I know it's too early to say anything yet, while you're smarting and hurt from that man's behaviour. But I want you to remember this and try to get used to the idea. I love you as I never thought I could love any girl. I want you to marry me—one day when you've forgotten all this present hurt."

CHAPTER TWELVE

JAN STARED AT him in utter amazement.

"Marry you?" she gasped. "But you know you don't really mean that! You know you could never stick to one woman—you said so yourself!"

"But that was weeks ago," he pointed out. "I thought I couldn't. But then I got to know you well, and there's something so different about you. You can laugh with me; you can be angry with me and more outspoken than anyone else has dared to be. But under it all, there's—how can I put it? An integrity—a deep-rooted honesty——"

"Don't!" She colored a little under his scrutiny. "You make me sound utterly priggish and horrible. And, really, I'm so absolutely ordinary. I don't believe you, you know Luis."

"But you will; I'll prove it to you bit by bit. I'm not going to hurry you, but I'm going to make you love me in the end and I'm going to persuade you to marry me. And, just to show you that I mean it, now that you're free, I'm going to kiss you as I've always wanted to kiss you."

She was still feeling too dazed to resist; he drew her to him and kissed her with a long passionate searching. Then, quietly, he dropped his arms and moved away.

"You're tired out," he said, with a sudden change of manner. "Go and get some sleep—and remember you're very precious to me."

He walked away, leaving her standing by the table, looking at the litter of plates and glasses still upon it, but not seeing them at all. She did not know, quite, whether she was awake or asleep. Perhaps she was dreaming all this; it was odd and unexpected enough to be a dream.

In the doorway, Luis almost cannoned into Nicolas, who was standing watching him with a scowl.

"Sorry if I eavesdropped," he said, turning to walk back with Luis away from the hospital. "I couldn't very well help hearing—and seeing. I think you're going too far, Luis.

You're a man of the world, with plenty of experience of women, and Jan's in my charge. A girl like that might have her head turned by a chap like you, but haven't you forgotten that she's engaged to a man at home?"

Luis smiled pleasantly.

"No," he said. "I hadn't forgotten. And there is no longer a man in England. If there had been, I should have kept quiet."

"I don't understand," Nicolas put in curtly.

"No? Well, use your brain a little. There was a mail from England today, no? Little Jan received a letter from that conceited brute breaking off the engagement because she is not important enough for him. Important! She, who has something he could search the world over for and not find in anyone else! I think I am not breaking a confidence in telling you this, for I wish you to understand. You see, I believe she is already a little bit in love with me and before long she will be much more so. She is going to marry me, Dr. Nick. Later on, of course, when she has got over the shock of that cad's behaviour and has convinced herself that, in this, she can trust me."

Nicolas' frown drew his brows together. His first look had been one of amazement and distress, but it was followed now by one that seemed almost of anger, as, lower lip a little out-thrust, he listened to Luis' speech.

"But can she?" he asked at last. "Trust you, I mean. She must be badly hurt now, and if you——"

Luis' eyebrows rose and he stiffened, becoming, of a sudden, very much the "grand seigneur."

"Certainly she can trust me," he replied coolly. "There is no reason why I should discuss the affairs of my heart with you, my good doctor, but I can assure you that, once married to me, Jan will have no cause for complaint. It appears too, that I must unwillingly remind you that I am not at all a match to be sneered at. Jan shall have everything she wishes and I shall consult her in everything. She will live where it pleases her, travel when she wants, have clothes and jewellery that I dare say she has never even dreamed of possessing."

Nicolas flushed a slow, angry red. He was not the sort of man to take such contemptuous condenscension easily, but just now he had other things upon his mind. Things which necessitated his keeping his temper. So he answered shortly, hiding his feelings. "Of course you can give her far more worldly advantages than anyone else, and she would have a very high position socially, married to you. But that sort of thing isn't much use without loving-kindness and mutual trust. You have only to read the number of smashed marriages among people who are just as rich as you to see that. And a girl like Jan would want a lot more than money and clothes to make her happy."

"So you do not trust me, either?" Luis cocked one eyebrow. "And yet this time I am serious. I will give her—if you wish me to put it into words—my love, once and forever."

He paused and then shot Nicolas a quick, maliciously mischievous smile.

"But it seems to me that you are taking an unreasonable interest in her affairs," he went on. "After all, they are entirely between Jan and myself. Of course, I understand that you are jealous——"

"Jealous!" Nicolas bit into his words. He was so furious that he never even heard Luis end his sentence with, "But I look upon it as a quite unpardonable intrusion into my private business and I shall be glad if you will keep out of it in future."

Before he had finished, Nicolas had turned upon his heel and walked away towards the hospital. He was seething with anger. Jealousy! Just because he felt responsible for the girl in his charge! After all, she was very young, and her hospital training and life at home could not have fitted her for meeting a man of the world like Luis on his own footing. She must have been badly hurt by Roderick, and if Luis were to hurt her again—— But as for jealousy! His thoughts ran on in unfinished sentences.

But why, he found himself wondering, should he feel it was such a catastrophe that Luis should want to marry her? He did, but what was the reason for it? Knowledge that constancy had never been one of Luis' virtures? But he had made no secret of that; Jan must have known it herself. And, if he really had fallen lastingly in love with her—well, they said the reformed rake made the best husband.

Personal dislike and distrust of the man? Well, to be strictly fair, how much of that was due to their friction on the island? If Luis had not wanted to buy Golden Grove and been ready to go to extreme lengths to obtain it, what would he have thought of him? And—again being strictly impartial—although his methods verged on the unscrupulous, they were all in the way of business, and Nicolas had to admit that he knew a number of highly respectable and trusted business-men whose methods were as sharp and who dismissed it all as being the expected thing in their world. No; Nicolas had really nothing definite against him. And, in a worldly sense, it would certainly be a wonderful marriage for Jan. However much he privately disliked the idea, he must stand on one side in this, preserving a strict neutrality. For Jan's own sake.

He walked back to the hospital. By now, Jan had managed to collect all the plates and glasses and carry them out to the kitchen, where she was washing them up with a dazed look on her face. She still could not quite believe the interview she had had with Luis. He couldn't want to marry her—it was quite impossible!

Nicolas came quietly into the room, picked up a tea-towel and started to dry.

"Quite time you'd finished and gone to rest," he said. "We'll just do these and leave the rest for Lily to finish off whenever she has time. You've had quite a day of it today, haven't you?"

She turned to look at him quickly, catching her breath, and he nodded a reply to her unspoken question.

"I've heard," he said quietly. "Luis told me. I'm sorry, Jan."

She blinked away weak tears of weariness.

"I'm trying to forget," she said in a stifled voice. "I don't suppose I can straight away. Just now I feel as though I never shall. But I want to work very hard and then there won't be time to think. I've got to be sensible. I'm not the first girl who has been jilted, and I expect all the others felt as I do at first and then got over it. And I've got my work——"

He felt inexpressibly touched by the white strained face, the courageous tilt of her head, the difficult slur of words that caused her such an effort to bring out. She was brave, he told himself; she had grit and endurance, and, one day, she would win through. Though that, he knew, did not make today any easier to bear.

"My dear," he said gently, "I've heard it said that a man—or woman—can be in love time after time, but they love only once. That is irreplaceable and lasts forever. The trouble is that being in love seems just like the real love at the time. It's afterwards that you see the difference—when real love comes. And I believe that your feeling for Roderick was just one of the 'in loves' that will pass. And, one day, you'll find the other."

She turned to look at him, her face startled. Her lips were open a little; she had not expected such words from him. Yet they were true, she knew; her work as a nurse had shown her that. But how did he know? Had he found the one love of his life—a love that would never die? For little Sarah-Ann? Had he seen beneath her childish mannerisms to a depth of character Jan did not know, and did he love that with an eternal love? She looked at him in silence, seeing him for the first time, neither as a clever and interesting colleague nor as a potentially good friend, but as a man who could love and suffer and feel the joy Jan had felt with Roderick.

"I—don't want anyone to know," she said at last. "Not yet. It would only make it harder."

"No one shall know from me," he assured her. "And I think we can trust Luis to keep quiet. Telling me was an exception."

Then, with a sudden change of manner, he took the mop with which Jan had been washing the china out of her hand.

"Now, go across to the house and straight to bed," he commanded her. "I'll give you something to make you sleep. No, it's no use saying you never take anything, because today you're going to. You won't be able to work properly tomorrow unless you get a good night's rest. I'm going to have a look at Mortimer and I can doss down on a bed here tonight. You're not to think of anything or anybody till tomorrow morning. Understand?"

She nodded, and then, with Nicolas propelling her by the arm, she walked across to the house, too tired and too bewildered by all the events of the day even to think properly. Tomorrow would be another day; it would have to be met with resolution and courage. But Nicolas would help her. And Luis. Did Luis really love her? Love her for always?

CHAPTER THIRTEEN

DAYS SLID INTO WEEKS almost unnoticed. Life had become a pattern. Things that had seemed so strange to Jan when first she came to Dream Island now seemed as if they had always been. The heat, the blaze of tropical color, the mud huts with their thatched roofs and banana trees in the garden, the never-ending soundfulness—ceaseless cries and murmurs of insect, animal and bird life, noise of the laughter, the shouting, the singing of the workers on the estate, the lapping of the sea at the foot of the cliffs—all these had woven themselves into her life as though she were a part of it.

She went to tea with the Andersons and enjoyed her visits. She liked big, bluff, rugged Joe Anderson, with his admiration of and deep love for his young daughter. She got to know Garth Owen better and, discovered his inarticulate devotion for Sarah-Ann, stifled a sigh for him. For Sarah-Ann was constantly with Nicolas now and, starry-eyed and glowing, could talk of nothing and no one else to Jan. Not that Nicolas showed his feelings for her openly, but he would never do that, Jan thought; he was too reserved. But there was a confidence and affection, a closeness of comradeship that, to the two girls, meant only one thing.

Griselda recovered quickly enough in a physical sense, but her spirits only seemed to sink the lower. She moped she snapped at everyone, she treated Leslie to alternate tantrums and displays of overwhelming repentance. It was not easy for Jan, who was struggling to push her own private feelings into the background, and more than once she decided that Griselda needed a good smacking and she wished she could be the one to administer it. She kept her patience with difficulty, however, and tried one thing after another to interest the mistress of Golden Grove, but all her ingenuity seemed to be taken up in making life miserable for as many people as possible, and Jan could only set her lips and make up her mind that Griselda must be jerked out of her present mood somehow or other.

Of course, Luis might have had something to do with it, for Jan was certain that he was not seeing Griselda alone now. Uncertain though she was about him, Jan had to admit that she could scarcely have got through those terrible days without the unfailing, if unspoken, sympathy he gave her, and the ways he thought out of keeping her amused.

For the first few weeks had been worse than anything Jan had ever known. The fact that she had not seen Roderick for some weeks did not make it any easier. Her whole life had been wrapped up in his, her whole future was part of his. She had thought of him, dreamed of him, longed for him. And now, part of her life had been broken roughly, hastily across. She was determined that no one but Luis and Nicolas must know, so she managed somehow to laugh and talk as usual, to be interested in all the little things of life that surrounded her; she managed to push the thoughts of Roderick to the back of her mind. But she had to admit, even though it was rather unwillingly, that she would have found it much more difficult without Nicolas' quiet, dependable presence and Luis' charm, and the moonlight barbecues, the trips and the amusements he arranged for her. Always with other people there, but with her openly as guest of honor.

She was working in the hospital one day when Bella West, the most enthusiastic member of their weekly clinic, came in at the door.

"Nurse, I've come," she announced. "It's early."

Jan gave one glance at her face, green-tinged with pain, and hurriedly rushed round to prepare a bed and call for Lily and boiling water. Nicolas was out; he had been called to a small hut perched on the cliff at the other end of the island. The man there had been injured in an accident and Nicolas had taken first-aid kit and hoped to bring him back to the hospital in his car. So Jan was left alone to bring the first baby to be born in the hospital into the world.

It gave her a wonderful sense of achievement to bath the tiny scamp and hand it to its mother. She had done her midwifery course, but here, in this far-off island, in the tiny primitive hospital, she felt a glow she had never known before as she remembered that, if it had not been for Nicolas and herself, some unskilled and probably dirty midwife would have brought the baby into the world, possibly with untold harm to the mother, who had had a difficult enough time as it was.

Bella crooned over her baby daughter.

"We'll call her Janet," she announced. "Me and my man talked it over and we said, Janet for a girl or Nicolas for a boy. And so everyone ought to who has her baby here, as I've been telling them all."

Jan laughed at the idea of the island populated almost entirely by little Janets and little Nicolases. But she was pleased and touched, too.

"I'm proud to have her called after me," she said softly, touching the velvety skin with a gentle finger.

After that, visiting hours, which had always been a problem, became almost an impossibility. Jan found it absolutely beyond her power to make them understand that certain times must be kept to. Friends, relatives and children flocked in from the moment that Jan, who was now sleeping in the hospital, got up in the morning until she had to turn them out almost by force to settle Bella off to sleep at night. Baby Janet, being the first baby on the island to be born in a hospital, was something of a celebrity and there was no way at all of stopping them.

"You're almost the only person who hasn't been," Jan told Griselda. "Why don't you visit her? She's quite sweet."

"Such a fuss about a baby!" Griselda snorted contemptuously. "You might think there'd never been one before! I hate all this silly sentimentality. But I can see through you, of course; you imagine that if I see one infant, I'll go all sloppy and earnest-minded and want to do welfare work with them all. Well, I won't, and I loathe kids, so you can get that idea out of your head!"

Since such a hope had, indeed, been at the back of Jan's mind, she changed the subject and, deciding that another faint hope had proved futile, returned to the hospital.

She arrived just in time to see Luis standing in the doorway, his arms piled full of woolly rabbits, dolls and mechanical toys of every kind.

"For the famous baby," he told her, dropping half of them on the floor and fumbling with the rest, managing to look as thoroughly uncomfortable and out of place as anyone could do. "I had them flown from Jamaica to show there's no ill feeling about the hospital."

"Oh, Luis!" Jan was torn between laughter and a new warmth. It was the first time she had looked upon him as someone capable of being as absurd and ridiculous as the rest of them, and this brought her much nearer to him.

"You're a darling to think of it," she went on. "But it'll be months before the baby can play with toys like that."

"Will it?" He rubbed his head ruefully. "I don't know anything about the little beggars. But I'm getting into practice for the time when I have some of my own. Do you not think I should make a good father, Jan?"

It was the first time he had even obliquely referred to the words he had spoken on the day of Roderick's letter, and she was not ready for it yet. She reddened a little and tried desperately to think of some way in which to change the subject. So it was a relief to see Nicolas coming towards them.

He gave the barest nod to Luis before he turned to Jan to say with unusual curtness, "An emergency, Jan. It'll mean an immediate operation, I'm afraid. Are you ready?"

Jan nodded. The case must be a serious one, she judged from the tense look on his face. She turned to Luis, picking up the last toy and balancing it precariously on top of the others as she said, "Thanks so much for the toys. Give them to Bella yourself, will you? She'll be in the seventh heaven at so much fame!"

"But—but I don't know what on earth to say to a baby," he protested helplessly.

His crestfallen appearance was almost ludicrous. He had had different ideas in his head when he had brought the toys across to the hospital, and he was not used to being brushed aside with such indifference. But Jan, tucking her hair more securely under her cap as she jog-trotted along by Nicolas' side in an effort to keep up with his huge strides, never even noticed Luis' attempts to detain her.

As soon as they reached the makeshift theatre, Nicolas turned to her with no attempt now to conceal his anxiety.

"It's Sophia White—Bill's wife," he said. "She has been ill for a long time, apparently, but never said a word to anyone about it till now, when she has collapsed. It's some sort of obstruction and it's going to be a big and long operation. And we're not properly equipped for it. But it must be done at once. No time to send her to one of the other islands."

"We'll do it." Jan pretended an assurance she was very far from feeling. Her hands had grown dry and she was having difficulty with her breathing at the very thought of the responsibility that would be hers. But she was determined not to add doubts of her capabilities to Nicolas' other worries, and she even managed to bring out in what seemed to her own ears quite an ordinary sort of voice, "Do you want me to give the anaesthetic again?"

"You'll have to." His answer was flat and unflattering. "Can you go and get her ready and then bring her in? Sorry so much has fallen on your shoulders."

"It's what I'm here for," she reminded him; she had not the heart to point out that when she came here, the last thing she had expected was to be nurse, cook, housemaid, district visitor and, on top of it all, anaesthetist. If only she didn't let him down! She prayed soundlessly while she prepared the woman, who seemed nothing but skin and bone and as tiny as a britle piece of china; there seemed nothing else to do.

Sophia was in bad health. Jan was not at all happy about the state of her heart; even in a large modern hospital a major operation like this would be a very big risk. Here —— But she wouldn't think about it; nothing was impossible. Her face was impassive as she scrubbed up and donned her surgical gown and mask.

Even now, through all her worry, she was able to admire the brilliant precision of Nicolas' surgery. He was as aware as she that the elderly woman would not be able to stand very much of it and he was working against time, but with a surety of touch that made him a joy to work with. But Sophia's breathing was erratic; her pulse almost imperceptible. And then, suddenly, Jan found that nothing she could do to keep her going was any use.

"I'm afraid——" she faltered. "I think her heart has stopped beating."

Nicolas gritted an exclamation under his breath. His instructions were brief and hurried, but they were none of them any use. Sophia had died under the anaesthetic and at last he was forced to realize that there was nothing more they could do.

He finished his work in silence and then turned away from the pathetically tiny body on the table.

"If I'd taken Luis' offer, if we'd had a modern hospital with a full staff," he said in a voice that broke a little, "this mightn't have happened. I've thrown away her life because of my obstinacy."

"You haven't!" she cried fiercely, wanting to pull him out of his self-reproach, knowing that he must not allow that thought to fester within him. "You know you haven't! You know how they love to have you! There wasn't much chance for her from the beginning; you know that even in the most modern of hospitals it would have been touch and go. A case like this on the island will only come once in a blue moon."

She paused for a moment and then said, rather falteringly, because the fear had been nagging at the back of her mind all the time, "Was it my fault? Did I do anything wrong?"

He looked at her quickly. He had pulled off his mask and he ran his hand through his thick mop of hair.

"You were wonderful," he said quietly, and the very matter-of-fact tone of his voice made the compliment all the greater. "You've done more than I could have thought possible. I don't know what I should do without you, Jan."

She flushed with pleasure. They stood facing each other and, just for a moment, they seemed very near in heart. But then he moved away. His face was grey with fatigue; she knew that he was still blaming himself because he could have made the hospital so much more modern if he had agreed to Luis' terms; she knew she could do no more to comfort him. All the men on the estate were his friends; he knew all their life stories, their hopes and their fears. And now he had done this to one of them; there was nothing she could do to help.

"I'll have to go and tell Bill," he said, his voice flat with the dejection he was feeling. "They were a devoted couple. They've a crowd of orphaned grandchildren living with them too. I'll have to find someone to take charge of them for a time."

"Take them to Golden Grove." An idea came suddenly to Jan through all her low spirits. "Give them to Griselda to look after."

"Griselda!" He stared at her in horror. "She'd refuse even to look at them."

"Try it, anyway," Jan suggested. "It would give her something to do, and that's what she needs."

He looked doubtful.

"Sarah-Ann would be better for them," he said. "She would play with them and make them laugh and forget their troubles. Griselda would only hand them over to Lily."

And Jan knew that Sarah-Ann it would be. She could not imagine, as she set about the sad task of looking after the little old woman's body, why the thought of his turning to Sarah-Ann should distress her so. Only because everything had gone so terribly wrong, she thought.

Bill took it well.

"It wasn't Doctor's fault," he said, as he stood by his wife's side for the last time. "He did all he could and he's sad now. But he shouldn't be. We should be glad that she's happy in heaven. Only it was all no use; she might have died in bed with me to hold her hand. She'd have liked that, would Sophia; we was always together in life and she'd have liked me to have been with her when she went to live with the good Lord. But I reckon He had other ideas."

His simple faith was almost too much for Jan. She blinked hard and he turned to her, with a smile on the rugged face down which he could not keep his tears from falling.

"Don't worry, Missie. You're one of us now," he told her. "We couldn't do without you."

His words touched her. After he had gone, she stayed alone for a long time thinking. Life on the island, the hospital. All these were jumbled together. Luis could do so much for them all if he would do it in a disinterested spirit.

Would he? He could be so kind; so understanding to her.

She remembered Nicolas' words about love that came only once. Could it possibly have come to Luis like that? Could she trust him now? Could she begin to love him? There was so much they could do together here. The trouble was, everything seemed to get muddled together and motives became hidden beneath the disorder. What were her feelings? Was she beginning to love this new Luis or was she persuading herself into it because of all they could do together? She turned very thoughtfully to go across to Golden Grove.

CHAPTER FOURTEEN

SHE HAD BARELY reached the hospital entrance before Luis came towards her to meet her, putting his hand on her arm.

"My poor darling!" he said. "You don't mind my waiting for you here, do you? I couldn't let you go, tired and alone. I hate you having to put up with sordid sights like that. It's wrong—all wrong for you."

She shook her head wearily.

"Not sordid, only tragic," she said, her voice trailing off at the end from sheer weariness.

He was quick to see this and he put his arm protectively round her.

"Sweet! You're too tired even to talk," he told her repentantly. "And I've been bothering you! But I won't any more. I won't say a word. But I'm going to take you out in my car to blow away the blues. You can just lie back in your seat and let the fresh air blow on you and I won't worry you at all."

The idea was tempting. She had intended to undress and go to bed, but she knew that she would never sleep. Sarah-Ann had come to take over at the hospital, where Bella only needed company now, and there was no reason why she should not go. So she began to thank Luis for his offer, though she never had time to finish her words, for, at once, he took hold of her hands and drew her towards his car, which was already waiting under a tree.

It was as luxurious as everything belonging to him, and Jan was able to lie back under the opened roof and let the breeze play on her face and ruffle her hair as they sped soundlessly along.

Luis kept to his word and, after seeing that she was comfortable, did not speak at all as he drove right away from the three small estates to the very edge of the island. Here, the shore was rocky and the land above had only a thin stratum of earth over the rugged stone; compared with the lush, fertile land on the other end of the island, it was scarcely worth cultivating, and the steep rocks, stretching treacherously out to sea, made a harbor impossible. So it was quiet and still. The sky above was as blue and cloudless as elsewhere, but the sea, rushing against the rocks with its waves white-tipped, lacked the translucent quality of the smooth expanse of water at the other end of the island.

Luis stopped the car and lit cigarettes for himself and Jan. For a moment they sat silent; only a couple of large sea-birds whirled overhead, sharp beaks out-stretched. Then Luis opened the car door and, picking Jan up in his arms, deposited her on the rough ground outside.

"There—sniff the salt in the air!" he commanded her. "It seems more like real sea here, where it's wild and rough, than in the picture-postcard blueness of the other side of the island. Doesn't that do you good?"

He kept his arm round her and she did not try to move away. She was so tired and he was being so kind and understanding that she was content to feel his arm holding her.

"Look, sweet; do you feel able to talk now?" he asked, after a moment's silence. "I hadn't meant to say anything for a long time yet—I have been good, you must admit, haven't I? But since I heard about the terrible time you must have been through with that poor woman, I just can't keep quiet any more. With a staff of only you and Nicolas, it may happen again; you may have to do work you're neither qualified nor fitted to do, and it will just break your heart. Darling, please listen to me. By now you must have realized that I really meant what I said; that I'm serious about you and you alone. Won't you consider marrying me?"

The note of humility in his usually arrogant voice touched her; she would scarcely have been human if it had not given her a small thrill of triumph. But she stared ahead at the tumbling sea, refusing to look at him.

"I'm too tired to think, Luis," she confessed. "I might say yes now, just because you've been so good to me and I feel grateful. But when I'm feeling my old self, I might wish I hadn't. You can't want to marry me just because I've been doing work I'm afraid I made a mess of and I'm depressed and upset, and don't really know what I feel or what I want."

"Can't I?" For a moment the devil of mischief danced in his eyes. "I'd want to marry you, whatever you felt like! But this affair has brought things to a head. If only Nicolas had seen sense, he could have had all the staff he wanted and you wouldn't have had to do it. Perhaps, even, the old woman would still be alive. But, all the same, just think, darling, of all we could do together. I love you so much that I'm sure you love me a little. And if we were married, you could arrange everything about the hospital with Nicolas—staff, new apparatus and everything you want there. We'd build new houses for the workers and make a model place of the whole island. Even if Golden Grove didn't belong to me."

She turned now to look at him.

"More moral blackmail?" she asked.

He shook his head and smiled wryly.

"Not with you now, my pet," he answered. "I'm too much in love. I was only trying to put my case in the best light for me. That's only human, isn't it?"

There was a great deal in that, she had to admit, and the thought of all they could do gave her a small glow of excitement. But she ought not to decide now when fatigue and gratitude were swaying her backwards and forwards and she could not think clearly.

"Then, why don't you give the new hospital now without any strings attached?" she asked.

"My sweet!" he protested. "I'm only human. If I was a saint, perhaps I would, but I'm just fighting with all my weapons for the one girl in the world I want."

She looked at him with troubled eyes. Somehow his frank avowal that he was using all the weapons on his side to win her brought her much nearer to him than any pretence of wanting the good of the people would have done. But she did not want to decide yet.

While she was hesitating, however, he drew her to him and kissed her.

"I have settled matters for you," he told her gently but with an undertone of triumph. "You are going to marry me, soon, quite soon. At once if I had my way, but I will not be too impatient, I will wait till you are ready. As long as I have you some time."

He added, as he kissed her again, "I never thought that I would feel for any girl as I do for you. But right from the first I felt you were different. I didn't want to be serious; I tried to amuse myself with Griselda, but it was no use. And when I heard that you were free, I knew that you were the only woman for me and that, without you, I should never be quite happy."

"The one love," Jan said dreamily. She wished that the memory of Nicolas strong face did not come before her as she said the words that he had said to her. Nicolas was her employer and that was all there was to it. If he loved anyone, it was Sarah-Ann, and Jan certainly did not want things to be any different. No; Luis was right. He had made up her mind for her. She was so fond of him; she enjoyed his company; her earlier mistrust of him was almost forgotten now in the belief that his love for her, her presence with him would stop him from his former unscrupulousness.

"Very well, Luis, I'll marry you," she promised. And then, because she remembered her own uncertainty and thought of all he was open-handedly giving her, she added solemnly, "I'll try to make you a good wife."

"Poppet!" He kissed her quickly and fleetingly, his voice wry as he went on, "It's all on the other foot, I'm afraid. Will I make you a good husband?"

They turned, as by common consent, to go back to the car. On the way back to Golden Grove, Luis asked, "May I announce the engagement straight away? I've a special reason for wanting to."

"I suppose so," Jan agreed in a surprised voice. "Why?"

"You'll see," he told her mysteriously, and refused to say any more.

Jan walked on to the verandah at Golden Grove a little way ahead of him. As usual, the Duncarrons were gathered there, Griselda flicking over the pages of a magazine that had just arrived from England, Leslie busy with estate returns and Nicolas deep in a medical paper. Griselda looked up from her magazine and, without noticing Luis, called out, "Jan, look here! Have you seen this?"

Jan took the magazine. Before, even, she looked at the photograph Griselda pointed out, she knew what it would be. Griselda went on, her voice clear and spiteful, "You've been leading us up the garden path, pretending you were engaged to him! Or has he thrown you over? The other girl is certainly very charming."

Jan's hands were trembling so that she could scarcely hold the paper. She saw the headlines, "Brilliant young barrister to marry his chief's daughter," and her eyes slid down to the photo-ed face of Roderick, eyes smiling as he looked at the charming, if affected, face of the girl standing by his side. After the first shock which, indeed, had almost overwhelmed her, she found herself thinking, "I don't care! How extraordinary!" She had known it would happen and the actual event was almost a relief.

Nicolas looked up quickly. "What's that?" he asked sharply and, rising to his feet, came to stand by Jan's side. She looked up at him and then turned away from the expression in his eyes. He looked angry—furiously angry—protective and —something else; she did not know what it was, but she knew well enough that she must not even let herself think about it.

Luis stepped forward, however, and smiled blandly at them.

"Indeed, no, Griselda," he said softly, but his voice seemed almost a threat. "Jan never deceived you. Only they found they were not suited. Luckily for me, for Jan has consented to marry me."

A sudden complete silence greeted his words. Griselda's mouth slipped open a little in her amazement and she threw Jan one look full of vindictive spite. In a moment, Jan knew, she would find something particularly blistering to say.

Nicolas moved a little. Jan wanted to look at him, but somehow she could not. She knew that he had come to her to protect her from Griselda's bad-tempered digs at Roderick's engagement; she felt grateful to him and, suddenly, a sense of intense loss filled her as though she had let him down. But there was no reason for that; none at all.

Leslie was the first to speak, and his congratulations were stilted. He disliked Luis extremely, Jan knew, and his opinion of her was still tinged to a jaundiced hue by Griselda's accusations at the time of the yachting accident. But when at last Nicolas spoke, the warmth of his voice made up for his brother's coldness, even though he only said, "I hope you'll be very happy, Jan. You deserve to. Let's have a drink to celebrate."

As the men went into the house to fetch out drinks, Griselda leant forward.

"So much for everything you said to me!" she whispered. "You were after him yourself all the time! How much more despicable can you make yourself? Pretending you were thinking of Leslie and me, when all the time you were angling for him yourself! I shan't forget this!"

It was quite useless to tell her how mistaken she was. In any case, there was no time. The men returned and talk became general.

Long after Luis had gone and night had fallen with tropical quickness, Nicolas walked back to the hospital with Jan. For a moment, he was silent and then he said gently, "So it was only being in love last time, and this time it's the real thing?"

His voice was half a question, but Jan did not know how to answer it. To call out, "I don't know!" would be disloyal to Luis, and yet, for some reason unknown to her, she longed with all her heart to let Nicolas know the true muddle of her feelings.

She said at last, "I think Luis loves me with the one love."

"He'd better!" Nicolas spoke grimly. "If he doesn't treat you well, I'll come and punch him on the nose!"

They both laughed, though Jan queerly did not feel like laughing. She felt less like it still when Nicolas asked, "Will you want to leave the hospital soon? I suppose, as Luis' future wife, you won't want to stay on."

"I will!" she cried vehemently. "I wish I could stay always, but I know that won't be possible. But you won't need me later because you'll have plenty of nurses. Nicolas, you will let me do all the things for the hospital that we dreamed of, won't you? Luis says I may."

She was completely unprepared for Nicolas' reaction. He started back and his voice was full of anger as he retorted, "Do you think I would take anything from Luis—or from you? Do you think you can act the Lady Bountiful and look down on us? No, thank you; I'll manage the hospital on my own efforts. I don't need Luis' money at all."

CHAPTER FIFTEEN

FOR a moment, the shock of Nicolas' words was so great that Jan could not even move. She just stood still, her eyes widening and darkened by the hurt that, starting sharply in her heart, seemed now to be spreading all through her.

Why should he speak to her like this? Why should he talk as though it were unforgivable to ask to help him to make the dreams they had dreamed together come true? Could she, without knowing it, have been tactless, have said something he considered an insult? She felt raw and aching with the hurt he had given her and, to her horror, she felt a sob rise in her throat.

She shook her head to shake it away. She tried to speak, to explain to him, but she could only manage to say, "I didn't mean——We thought of everything together; I hoped we could carry it out together," and then her voice trailed miserably away.

His face changed suddenly; he looked at her as though he had never seen her before, and his voice was rough with concern as he answered her.

"I'm sorry. I don't know what came over me. Suddenly I saw what a fool I'd been and I was so furious with myself that I took it out on you. Why on earth didn't I realize before? And now it's too late!"

Jan had no idea what he was talking about. She supposed he himself knew what it was all about, but for the moment all that mattered to her was that he had not, after all, meant the words he had hurled at her in his rage. But she was still too startled by his reaction to her suggestion to do more than say uncertainly, "I didn't think you would mind. I thought you would be glad."

"Glad?" His lips twisted a little. "I ought to be, oughtn't I? I can't explain why I was suddenly so rude—not now. But I felt as though I hated Luis so much that I didn't want to be beholden to him for anything. But it won't do to say a thing like that to you, will it? Or you'll be hating me."

"No." She shook her head. "I couldn't do that. Ever. But we've got rather far away from the subject, haven't we?"

"Yes. And you've had such a disturbing day that you're to go straight to bed and sleep through the night. And those are doctor's orders, so no arguing!"

Quite obviously the subject was closed as far as he was concerned, and he pushed her towards the hospital and turned back towards the house. She was glad to carry out his orders. Sarah-Ann had conscientiously settled Bella off for the night, changed Baby Janet and tucked her in her cot by her mother's side. Jan looked into the little ward, but only Bella's heavy breathing disturbed the silence, so she hurried to her own bed, threw off her clothes and tried to sleep.

But so much had happened today that sleep evaded her. Instead, she started wondering about her promise to Luis. At one moment, she became almost panic-stricken about it and had to pull herself together to stop herself from jumping out of bed and rushing off to tell Luis straight away that it was all a mistake.

It wasn't, of course. She managed to calm herself. Luis had been wonderful to her lately and she had grown immensely fond of him. She had always found him a stimulating companion and she had felt a thrilled response to his practised love-making. So what on earth was she worrying about? Why, when she closed her eyes and tried to think of him, was it Nicolas' face that danced before her, the angry set of his mouth and harsh violence in his voice when first she had told him of her ideas about the hospital?

It was a long time before she drifted off to sleep, and she was still heavy-eyed when she got up next morning to find a regular mob of people outside, waiting to talk to her. Somehow the news of her engagement had already got round the whole island, and she was touched and delighted to find how completely she was treated as one of themselves.

All the same, her engagement did not appear to be as popular as she had hoped.

"Mas'r Corando ain't one of us," one of the women said outright. "You are, Nurse Jan. We wanted you to marry

Dr. Nick; we'd got it all settled. What you want to go and promise to marry the other one for? Can't you change it?"

Jan laughed and suddenly wanted to hug them all.

"I'm afraid not," she answered. "I expect Dr. Nicolas would be quite horrified at the idea, too; so what should I do then?"

"Little Miss Sarah-Ann's a nice chil'," the old woman replied, shaking her head. "But her too young for our Dr. Nick. No, you young folk go arrange it all wrong, but there's no telling you!"

So they, too, had noticed how the friendship between Nicolas and Sarah-Ann was growing and developing! Jan did not know why the warmth seemed to have gone a little out of the day, and she was not sure what rejoinder she made. Sarah-Ann herself made a diversion, however, by arriving with a horde of the White grandchildren trailing along behind her.

"Will you want me this morning, Jan?" she asked. "I thought I'd take the crowd here down on the beach if not."

"I can manage," Jan told her. "But won't they be too much of a responsibility? How many of them are there?"

"Eight," Sarah-Ann laughed. "The oldest is ten and the youngest two. But don't bother; as long as I keep an eye on the baby, the older ones will look after themselves. They all swim like fishes, anyway, so they can't drown!"

The smile lingered on Jan's lips as she returned to the hospital and opened the surgery ready for the odd cases who came to see Nicolas. How surprisingly Sarah-Ann had developed lately! She seemed to have grown up quite suddenly; her silliness had left her and a new strength of character come to light. As she had walked towards the beach the dark-skinned, kinky-haired children had been dancing round her, clutching her hand, fighting for her attention and quite obviously loving her. She would make Nicolas a wonderful wife. It was absloutely absurd of Jan to have that niggling feeling that she didn't want that to happen.

The surgery was an especially busy one that morning. Not, Jan suspected, because more people had anything wrong with them, but because they all wanted to see her in her new role of fiancée to the great Luis Corando. So she and Nicolas were kept busy, while Leslie had ridden out to a canefield which seemed to be developing less well than they had hoped.

Griselda waited till the house was empty; then she went to her room and changed out of the housecoat she was wearing into a jade-green dress that matched her eyes. She took particular care over the arrangement of her hair, and then made up slowly and attentively.

There were small wrinkles round her eyes and her lips dropped petulantly.

"Bother this climate!" she said aloud to herself. "It makes me look an old hag! But, surely, even now I can compete with Jan!"

Her feelings about Jan were complex. As an individual, she liked her very much, and if she had been downright hideous—or even uninterestingly plain—she would have been glad to make a friend of her. As it was, at one moment she felt overwhelmed with jealousy of her because she was young and fresh and full of a keen zest for life and because men seemed to find her worth looking at, even though she herself seemed unaware of the fact. At these times, Griselda felt spitefully vindictive and would have done anything to hurt her. It just wasn't fair that Jan should have so much when she was quite content to be a nurse, while Griselda, who felt she needed admiration and enjoyment as a flower needs air and moisture, was tied to an unreasonable husband in a dead-and-alive hole whose one and only celebrity had turned towards Jan instead of continuing to run after Griselda. She brooded on the unfairness of it all and felt she hated the young nurse.

Then reaction would set in. She would remember how kind Jan had been to her, how she had put herself out to amuse and interest Griselda in spite of snubs and rudeness, and then she would be overwhelmed with remorse and would decide to be as nice as she possibly could and make up for everything.

But Jan's engagement had made her forget all her good resolutions. Jan was sly and underhand, she decided; she had set out from the very first to catch Luis. She must have known that when he could get any girl so easily, the best way to arouse and keep his interest was by holding back herself. He would have been content to make love to Griselda in quite a mild and respectable sort of way if it hadn't been for Jan's tactics. Griselda was so filled with fury that she knew only a determination to get her own back.

So, now that the coast was clear, she got ready, and when at last she was more or less satisfied with her appearance she set off for the Corando house.

Luis was out in the stables, examining a chestnut mare which had been giving some trouble.

"See," he pointed out to Griselda, "I call her Grisel after you, because you are both beautiful and graceful and her hair is a pale imitation of yours. But she is a woman and perverse, and we have had much trouble with her lately. You, I hope, are not going to follow her example?"

"And give you trouble?" Griselda's green eyes flashed. "So you admit that I've reason for it?"

He shrugged his shoulders, throwing her a mischievous, surprised look.

"But no! why should you have?" he asked. "It is merely from the symptoms. A — shall we say a militant air, a certain brightness of the eyes and pursing of the lips. Oh, yes, I know well enough when a lady is cross with me but, in this case, I cannot think of any reason."

"Can't you?" She spoke abruptly. When it came to a passage of wits, Luis was always the winner because he kept cool and slightly, aloofly amused, while her temper and her feelings ran away with her. "Can't we go somewhere to talk?" she finished curtly.

"But of course! I forgot my manners. Pray forgive me." He jumped smartly to attention. "Let us go into the house and you shall have a drink. You must need one after that hot walk."

But she was not at all disposed to make polite conversation. Griselda had always been a person of one idea, and now the one burning longing in her mind—to do something to get her own back on Jan—would not allow her any other thought. So she shrugged her thin shoulders petulantly as she walked towards the house and did not speak until he had handed her a long drink with the ice clinking in the glass.

Then she said sharply, "You're very trusting, aren't you? It isn't like you to stand by and watch yourself being made a fool of."

He raised his eyebrows questioningly, but when he spoke his voice was cold and quiet—so cold and quiet that it sounded dangerous, and, even through her anger, a small shiver of fear ran down Griselda's spine.

"I believe I do not understand you," he said, icily polite. "In fact, I prefer not to understand you. I think the implication is an insult both to me and—to someone else who is even more important to me."

"I don't care!" she burst out hotly. "You can't do anything to me. You can only glare as if you wanted to turn me into a pillar of stone, but it's worth it. Because you're being fooled—utterly fooled! Why do you think Jan is so keen on staying on at the hospital? What does she do there, all the time when she's alone with Nicolas?"

"She works," Luis answered nonchalantly. "You're a little fool, aren't you, Griselda? Your jealousy is as obvious and as green as your eyes. But, my dear, allow me to remind you that you've no real cause for complaint. There has never been anything between us but a few pretty speeches and one or two not-too-ardent kisses, and you have known from the first that it meant nothing to me—nor, I am sure, to you. I know I am every sort of a rotter but I do not willingly lead astray a married woman. You knew, too, from the first that Jan was different."

She swallowed, trying to push back the rage that seemed likely to overpower her altogether. She must keep her self-control or she would get nowhere at all with him.

"I know all that and I'm not grumbling," she managed, untruthfully, to say. "But you forget that I see Jan every day. We talk as women do when they're together without men, so I know a side of her that you don't. She's in love with Nick—she always has been. But she didn't manage to get him, so she turned to you. You've got money; actually to be fair, I think that only matters to her in terms of what she can do for the hospital. But doesn't that in itself show you? She would do anything for Nicolas. Why, even all the workers have seen it. When they heard of her engagement to you, they all said that you had only caught her on the rebound because Nick is so wrapped up in that silly little Sarah-Ann now. But he's only human, you know. And the unattainable is always the most precious. When they're alone together in the hospital, working close to each other, with the same aims and ideals, what do you think will happen if you go on being an ostrich?"

"I think," he said slowly and deliberately, "that you have already said too much. There are things, Griselda, that I cannot forgive. And you are a woman and have been my friend, so I think it would be best for you to go at once before I say anything I might regret later."

She crimsoned and bit her lip, but there was nothing else for it. She had to get up without having accomplished the smallest part of all she had come here to do. She hated him at that moment; she hated Jan. Almost, in her fury, she hated herself. But she would not, if she could help it, let him see that he had had the better of her. This was not the time for the nerve storm she would have loved to indulge in.

So, instead of giving way, she walked somewhat unsteadily towards the door, but there she turned round to face him with her last shot.

"Jan's marrying you soon," she said. "If I've been talking complete nonsense, she'll leave the hospital if you ask her, specially if you promise to send for another nurse to take her place. Try that and see what she says. If she agrees to leave, I'll take back all my words and apologize. But, somehow, I don't think I'll have to."

And, conscious of having had the last word, she swept out of the room with more dignity than she had believed possible.

CHAPTER SIXTEEN

SURGERY LASTED FOR a long time that morning, and the complaints the patients brought with them became more and more obviously a mere excuse for a chat with their newly engaged nurse. At last, Nicolas went to the door and shooed them all away.

"If anyone is really ill, he can come and see me alone this afternoon," he announced. "But the surgery hour isn't the place for a social gathering. So I want the place cleared within three minutes."

At the unexpected note of command in his voice, the crowd scattered. The men to the work they should have been at many hours ago; the women, most of them, to visit Bella and to turn the wonderful piece of news over and yet over again amongst themselves.

Nicolas got up from the desk and stretched himself.

"Well, thank goodness that's over!" he said. "If you will become a celebrity overnight, you see what you let yourself in for on the island! Can you clear up here, and then will you go to Brown Gully to see old Moses Lawson? The old chap's not at all well. I ordered him to bed and told him you'd be along to make him comfortable during the morning. I've got to go to the Weston family at the other end of the island. The conditions there are a disgrace. Can't you get any idea of cleanliness into their heads?"

"I went down on my knees and scrubbed their floor and then I stood over Mirabelle and watched her do it all over again," Jan told him. "I bullied and chivvied her into cleaning the whole place out and washing their clothes and bedding and I showed her how to cook. She promised me with tears in her eyes that she was a reformed character and would do everything I'd shown her. But that was a fortnight ago."

Nicolas laughed.

"And Mirabelle Weston's good intentions never last longer than three days," he agreed. "Well, in a way I suppose we can't blame her. With a lazy good-for-nothing husband who spends all his money on drink, and ten children, it would take a good deal of strength of will—and body—to have things spotless for them. I'm sorry, Jan; did I snap at you about it? I'm worried about Isaac Weston, though. He has always been a weak, shifty, idle fellow and not too strong in the head, and now he seems to have got in with the trouble-makers who promised him the world and no work if he joins them—which, of course, is his idea of paradise."

"Are they still making trouble?" Jan asked quickly. "I thought, after you called them all together and talked to them and pointed out that they wouldn't get more—probably much less—anywhere else, they quietened down."

"Yes, they have. I don't quite understand it." Nicolas' voice was worried. "I wish we had enough labor on the island without getting anyone else in. I know how to treat our own fellows and they know us, too. But this lot——"

He broke off and smiled at her.

"But this certainly won't get the work done!" he went on. "No need to worry till there's something to worry about. If you'll see Moses, then——"

He went out of the hospital and Jan set about tidying things up. Sarah-Ann was still with the children, but she could leave Bella now for half an hour. She was already getting up each day and would very soon be going home. So Jan was just ready to set out when the door opened and Luis came in.

"Oh, Luis!" she greeted him in surprise. "You know you shouldn't come here while I'm working! Or is anything wrong with you?"

"Yes, very wrong," he answered promptly, and laughed at the look of quick alarm on her face.

"No; it's nothing physical," he continued in reply to her hurried questions. "And I don't want to see Nicolas. In fact, he's the very last person I wish to see. The trouble, to help you to your diagnosis, is a particularly bad attack of love. I can't keep away from you, Jan."

"But you must when I'm working. That's very important," she told him. "Though you can walk with me as far as Moses Lawson's cottage if you want. I've got to see him. Then you must leave me alone till I'm off duty."

"Which is practically never," he reminded her, as they started to walk away from the hospital towards the part of the island known as Brown Gully. "What's the use of being engaged when I can never see anything of my fiancée? You think more of the hospital than anyone or anything else."

She looked at him with her eyes troubled.

"But it is my work, you know," she reminded him. "You wouldn't expect me to neglect it, would you? Besides, I do get a lot of free time unless an emergency crops up."

"And you never know when that's going to be," he retorted. "We can never arrange anything, because at the last moment there may be an accident or something. Even if we do go out, you insist upon leaving word where you're going in case you're needed."

"But it's always been the same," she protested. "You knew it would be and you've never said anything about it before."

"Because I'd no right to," he answered. "Now I'm engaged to you. We're going to be married soon and we ought to see something of each other before that happens. Don't you agree?"

"Of course. But there's time." Her voice sounded distressed and anxious. "We shan't be married as soon as all that."

"Shan't we?" His eyes narrowed and he scrutinized her face, a little flushed now, her eyes worried and preoccupied. What he saw made his lips tighten.

But he took hold of her arm and walked along companionably by her side. His voice was still pleasant as he said, "Look here, my pet. I don't like the girl I'm going to marry having to work like this. Besides, you've your trousseau to get and all sorts of other things, and I expect you'll want to see your parents. Leave the hospital. You could fly to Jamaica, and your mother and father could come out there. As my guests, of course."

She stopped short in her surprise and turned round to face him. Her face was full of amazement and gratitude, but there was consternation there too.

"But I couldn't possibly!" she exclaimed. "It's sweet of you to think of it, Luis. To remember my parents like that, I mean. You seem to get nicer and nicer every day. But

Daddy couldn't leave his practice, just like that. And I'm sure Mummy wouldn't come without him. Besides, in any case, I couldn't leave the hospital; I'm needed there, you see."

"My poppet!" He laughed and rubbed his hand gently against her cheek. "You've got rather a good opinion of yourself, haven't you? You're not the only nurse in the world, you know! No, I wouldn't dream of expecting you to leave them in the lurch. But if I pay for another nurse to come out to take your place, there's no reason on earth why you shouldn't leave."

"But—but——" Jan faltered over the words. "She wouldn't know—she wouldn't understand the people. I'm only just beginning to. Besides, I promised Nicolas."

"And that means more to you than I do?" he asked coldly.

"No—oh, no! Please understand!" Her voice sounded desperate. "You know what I feel about you. I told you everything yesterday. But this isn't just an ordinary job that can be filled at a moment's notice. It'll take time to find exactly the right person, and then she ought to come out here and work with me for some time to get the hang of things before I leave. I can't just walk out and hope that things will be all right. Please, Luis! Do try to understand!"

He flinched a little beneath the vibrant earnestness of her voice. Then he put his hands on her shoulders and pulled her gently round to face him.

"Very well, my dear," he said, as he looked down into her flushed, distressed face. "As I told you yesterday, you're different from all the other girls I know, so I must take your word for it and trust you. But all the same"—his tone changed and became full of passion; he caught her suddenly to him and kissed her violently—"all the same, I'm going to marry you. Whatever happens; I shall never let you get out of it. You're the one thing I've wanted forever and I'm going to have you. Understand?"

She pulled herself away from him, looking at him in surprise and with an unexpected dignity.

"I don't think you had any need to say all that," she told him quietly. "I haven't given you any reason to think I'm trying to get out of it. I don't want to. I haven't wanted to, though when you behave in that sort of way, you make me wonder why. It's as if you don't trust me."

"Dearest!" His voice changed again to one of tenderness. "I'm sorry. It's jealousy. I want you all the time. I want you to think only of me, to worry only about me, to wish to please only me. But I know that's unreasonable. And I do trust you, precious. You're the one—the only—person in the world I believe in utterly."

He saluted her quickly and then walked away without giving her time to answer. Not that she knew quite what to say, in any case. His sudden outburst had both surprised and perplexed her and, added to this, she had a guilty feeling that, though her words to him had been true as far as they went, they were not quite the whole truth. She didn't want to leave the hospital. Not only because of the difficulty in getting a nurse to fit in, but because she enjoyed it so much that she hated the thought of going from it. When he complained about the upset of their many plans, she had realized somewhat guiltily, that she hadn't minded at all. Because the people were so interesting to her, the work amongst them so engrossing that she was absolutely happy in it.

So she stood watching him as he walked away, wondering what she could do to make it up to him and how she could make him matter more to her than the hospital. He turned the corner as she watched and, from here, on the brow of the hill, she looked down, instead, to the cliff path. Sarah-Ann was toiling up it, pushed from behind by one child while another tugged at her from the front. They were all roaring with laughter and, as Jan watched, she saw Sarah-Ann give a lurch and almost fall. This seemed to be an intensely comic event; they all stood still to double themselves up with mirth. Jan waved and then went on towards the little house on Brown Gully.

Sarah-Ann was thoroughly enjoying her morning. She was near enough to the age of the older children to join in their games and answer their schoolboy badinage in kind. She decided, as she shepherded them all towards their grandfather's house, that when she and Nicolas were married she would start a children's nursery where mothers could leave their infants once a week to give them a rest from the constant round of housework, child-bearing and looking after the children already in the world. By now, in her thoughts, she always said "*when*" she married Nick, not, as formerly, "If" she married him. They seemed so close that, although he had never kissed her and certainly never even mentioned love to her, she believed that he must feel as she did.

She thought of the few months that had passed since she had left school, and wondered at the way both she and things seemed to have changed. Was it only a month or so ago that the sum total of her desires was to hurl herself from one excitement to another? To indulge in tantrums when things did not go as she wanted, and to sulk openly and with considerable noise when she felt aggrieved?

She laughed and threw back her head. The sun was hot on it, and the breeze lifted her hair and blew it back upon her forehead. She felt suddenly, exultantly glad to be alive, to be a woman and to feel the strength in her arms and legs and the laughter bubbling up in her throat.

"I've grown up—all in a couple of months!" she cried aloud, to the amazed delight of the children, who gathered round her capering and pulling faces and chanting, "Missy Sarah-Ann's grown up!"

Whereupon she cast all dignity to the winds and chased them, squealing, towards the White's cottage.

"Now, go in and have your siestas and behave yourselves!" she adjured them sternly.

"Or the zombies will get us," they chorused in reply, and ran up the straggly garden path to the tiny thatched hut that seemed as if it could never hold so many people without bursting its walls.

Sarah-Ann turned away. As she walked slowly towards home, she saw Luis climbing the hill and stood still to watch him for a moment. He did not see her and his preoccupied and frowning expression surprised her.

He doesn't look much like the happy fiancé, she thought. Of course, he can be awfully charming when he wants, but I don't think he's nice enough for Jan, really. I hope he won't make her unhappy.

She was so busy thinking this, that, for a moment she did not notice him turn into one of the huts. When she realized where he had gone, she looked at the hut with a frown of surprise.

It belonged to Ben Grant—one of the newcomers to the island and the ringleader of the discontented element on the Meynall estate.

Whatever, she wondered, could Luis be doing there? It wasn't like him to take notice of the workmen at all, not even those on his own estate, so why should he trouble about the men who worked for Golden Grove?

It wasn't anything much, of course; there was probably some absolutely reasonable explanation. But, all the same, the small worry refused to be forgotten. He had looked so furious too. Perhaps furious was not the right word. There was a cold, angry vindictiveness about him that had been evident even from her distance. That was what had made her shiver and wonder whether Jan would ever be really happy with him.

But, of course, Garth Owen would know why Luis had visited the man. If there was nothing at all to disturb herself about, he would be able to tell her. Making up her mind, Sarah-Ann turned and walked hurriedly towards the small bungalow which was the home of Luis' manager. She would get to the bottom of the mystery and then she would feel satisfied.

CHAPTER SEVENTEEN

GARTH HAD JUST come in for his lunch when she arrived. It was badly cooked and served in a slovenly manner. Sarah-Ann, temporarily diverted from the reason for her visit, stood by the table, looking down at the stained cloth, the knives and forks thrown anyhow down upon it, the unappetizing fat meat—a grey mass in the middle of a pile of beans.

"Is this what Gertrude expects you to eat?" she asked. "You need a woman to look after you, my boy!"

Garth grinned at her, his pleasant face alight with welcome.

"Will you take it on?" he asked. "The situation's vacant if you care to apply."

"You're more than a full-time job," she retorted. "And I seem to have my hands full already. But I shall certainly tell Gertrude what I think of her before I go. No one but a man would put up with it! Giving you food like this and charging you for all she cooks and gives away to her nephews and nieces, I bet!"

"I need someone to look after me," he told her with mock pathos.

"You sure do—you great, helpless gorm!" she told him sitting down by the table and remembering suddenly why she had come to see him.

"Oh, I know!" she exclaimed. "I want to talk to you about Luis."

"I don't," he answered positively. "I see enough of him while I'm working for him. Can't we be interesting about ourselves instead?"

"No, we can't," she told him sternly. "I only came here to ask you about him, not for the pleasure of your company. I saw him going into Ben Grant's hut today. What would he want with him? Does Ben work for you now?"

"I should say not!" Garth replied emphatically. "I wouldn't have him for the world! And even if he did, Luis wouldn't be likely to see him. He leaves all the engaging of the men and that sort of thing to me and never interferes. I will say that for him. You must have been mistaken. It couldn't have been Luis."

Sarah-Ann did not answer this. She knew so certainly that it was, indeed, Luis that it was not worth wasting her breath about. Instead, she asked thoughtfully, "Ben is at the head of those trouble-makers, isn't he? I heard he was a paid agitator."

"Very likely. Ben Grant would do anything for money," Garth replied, but when she asked, "Who pays him, then?" he had no answer ready.

"Why bother about anyone so objectionable?" he asked. "It isn't often I have the pleasure of your company. Why spoil the short time we have together?"

"There's something about it that worries me." She ignored his words. "Something wrong—— Oh, well." She jumped to her feet and gave him a light pat on the top of his head. "Get on with your lunch, my child. *I* am going to scare the pants off that housekeeper of yours."

"No, stay and talk to me." He made a grab at her, but she eluded him without any difficulty and crossed the patio to the tiny kitchen quarters outside. Gertrude's conscience was uneasy and her face correspondingly sulky when "Missy Sarie-Ann" came marching towards her with the light of battle in her eyes. Not without cause, for she proceeded to tell the housekeeper what she thought of her cooking and her housekeeping abilities in general so forcibly that that good woman passed from injured protestations of innocence to truculence and on to tears and promises of amendment.

When she thought that she had impressed her sufficiently, Sarah-Ann left the bungalow and turned towards home. The glow of glory did not remain with her for long, however; her mind returned again and again to Luis' visit to Ben Grant and her certainty that it boded only harm to Nicolas. She turned the matter over and over in her mind till she determined to go to see Nicolas himself about it. Perhaps he would have some explanation to offer. If it had been anyone but Luis, it wouldn't have mattered so much, but Luis, with the careless remark that he did not keep a dog and bark himself, never went near any of the houses in the native villages. So why pick on Ben Grant of all people?

Lily, at Golden Grove, announced that Dr. Nick had not yet come back for lunch, but she had heard that he had gone across the island to "scare some sense into that poor trash, Mirabelle Weston." Sarah-Ann considered with satisfaction that her old ex-nannie, who ran their home, would perhaps scold if she arrived late for lunch, but would scurry round to provide her with a hot and appetizing one, whatever time it was. So she decided to walk to meet Nicolas and talk to him on their way home.

Nicolas was almost exploding with exasperation at the small, ramshackle hut belonging to Isaac Weston, his wife and large family. Whereas almost all the other shacks on the island, even if they were tumbledown and often insanitary, were well tended, with small, cultivated strips of garden, with their own banana trees, their own little patch of maize, their vegetables and usually an enclosure for two or three scraggy hens, Isaac's house was unashamedly tumbling down. There were great holes in the thatch through which rain, in the wet season, poured, flooding out the three small, dirty rooms which composed the whole of their dwelling. Huge cracks in the walls let in trailing tendrils of climbing plants, and spiders, iguanas and cockroaches indiscriminately made their homes in the crevices. Outside, a bare patch of earth was trodden into a hard brown playground in the dry season and a sea of mud in the rains. No plants grew here, no carefully tended fruit trees. Not even weeds could thrust their way through the cement-like-hardness of the neglected wilderness.

Nicolas examined the four-year-old child he had come to see, and then, with a sigh of exasperation, he turned to Mirabelle Weston.

"Do you know what's wrong with this child?" he asked fiercely.

Mirabelle's large, flabby body shook as she looked at his angry face. Her hair was falling loosely round a face bloated with the wrong sorts of food, whose only reminder of former good looks was her huge black eyes, rolling now in apprehension. Her dress was torn and dirty; the child wore only a tattered rag.

"No, Doctor," she said nervously. "That's why I asked you to come. Playing about just like all the others yesterday and today not able to keep a drop down. What's the matter, Doctor?"

"Neglect. Just sheer neglect," Nicolas snapped out. "If you have children, why can't you look after them?"

Tears coursed down Mirabelle's cheeks.

"I do try, Doctor," she assured Nicolas. "I love them little ones—every one of them. But there's so much work and I'm always tired and there's not enough money to buy good food for them. So what can I do?"

Nicolas' face softened a little.

"I know it's hard for you, Mirabelle," he told her. "But something has got to be done if you're to bring the children up at all. I know your life isn't easy, but the life of your children is worth an effort, isn't it?"

She wrung her hands, tears pouring down her cheeks.

"What am I to do, Doctor?" she asked.

He selected the chair which seemed least dirty and most solid, and sat down on it.

"First," he said, "Isaac gets as much pay as any of the other men with families of the same size. They keep their children clean and their homes decent. Whatever these paid agitators may tell you, I pay a higher rate than on most of the other islands, and you own your own cottage. If it was mine I should pull it down, but, as it isn't, you must make Isaac mend the cracks in the walls and re-thatch it. Then, insist upon getting your share of his pay. Perhaps I could arrange to have it paid straight to you so that you could take out all the children need before handing over his pocket-money. I can tell you this; he would be a great deal better off in health if he didn't spend so much on drink. Quite frankly, I'd have given him notice ages ago if it hadn't been for you and the children. He's the most idle, good-for-nothing rascal I've come across yet."

"Work don't agree with him," Mirabelle protested weakly.

Nicolas ignored her words as he went on, "And if you grew your own vegetables and maize and bananas as everyone else does, you would have fruit and so on just for the picking. You know my brother and I are always willing to provide young plants and seedlings free for anyone who wants them for their gardens."

"This soil's too hard," Mirabelle began to protest, but Nicolas broke into her words.

"Good heavens, woman," he exclaimed irritably, "it's just the same as everyone else's garden would be if they neglected theirs as you neglect this. Get your husband to dig it all up and water and manure it. The older children would help —give them something to do. Plants grow easily enough out here—almost too easily. Once the garden was prepared, you'd have no difficulty with it."

"But how am I to get Isaac to agree?" asked Mirabelle. "I know you're right, Doctor, but Isaac ain't strong, and when he comes in at night he needs his drop of drink and his rest."

Nicolas looked at her with pity. Feckless, ignorant and slatternly as she was, he knew that she honestly wanted to make a good home for the children and, married to a decent man, probably would have done so. He knew that her life was one long struggle against Isaac's drunkenness and its consequences to all of them, and that she had not the strength of will or character to fight. But he had struggled for years to help them with advice, charity and kindness. Now something more drastic must be done if the children were to survive their deplorable conditions.

So now he said with a sternness that made her wince, "Look here, Mirabelle, your Isaac is nothing but a drunken good-for-nothing and you know it. I've put up with it for long enough and now I've come to the end of my patience I've tried to help you; now you must help yourselves. Tell Isaac exactly what I've said and what I expect him to do. I shall come back here in a week's time and if he hasn't started on the repairs of the house and garden I shall have the children taken somewhere where they'll be properly looked after, and they'll stay there till you prove yourselves capable of giving them a proper home. Understand?"

Mirabelle was too overcome by the awfulness of this thought to answer at all. She started to rock backwards and forwards, making a keening sound. After giving an exasperated exclamation, Nicolas strode out of the hut. If he stayed, he would probably weaken and give her some encouragement, and that was not what she needed. She had had that both from him and from Jan so many times before and it had not worked. Now the only thing left to make her pull herself together was fear. So he left her on his last words, even though he could not help feeling ashamed of his manner and sorry for her bewildered terror.

He pulled the door of his car open sharply, to find Sarah-Ann curled up in the seat waiting for him.

"Hello," he said in surprise. "You look like an elf or something rather nice sitting curled up like that."

"And you look like an ogre with your face black and frowning," she told him, sliding into the farther seat. "Is it Mirabelle?"

"It's the whole set-up." He started the car and began to explain. It was a relief to get it off his chest. Sarah-Ann made a good little listener, sitting there all big eyes and quick wit. But today she seemed to be less wide awake than usual; as if she had something else on her mind, and at last, when she had murmured, "I'm sure you're right, Nick. Something had got to be done," without her usual whole-hearted championship or equally whole-hearted disagreement, he broke off and turned to look at her again.

"What's wrong, Sarie?" he asked. "Something is, isn't it?"

"It may be or it may not," she replied cryptically. "It's just worrying."

She told him about the cold, devastating anger on Luis' face when she had seen him and went on to mention his visit to Ben Grant.

"That's what worries me," she explained. "He never visits the men. I feel there must be something wrong when he goes to the one man who's out to make mischief. Nick—why is Ben trying to make trouble? I've heard people say that he's a paid agitator, just here to stir up labor trouble among the workers. But, if so, who's paying him? Nick"—her face was pale and her voice earnest— "it can't be Luis, can it? But if so, why? Why should he want to make trouble here?"

Nicolas stopped the car. His face was thoughtful and frowning, and the hand on the steering-wheel clenched itself into a fist.

"I thought that once," he admitted. "I thought he was trying to force Leslie and me into selling Golden Grove to him. But lately I decided I must have misjudged him. Since he fell in love with Jan, he seems to have become a much nicer person. For he is in love with her, you know."

"I know." Sarah-Ann drew her breath in sharply. "And I'm afraid of that, too, Nicolas. If you'd seen his face—the cruel look on it. What if he isn't nice to Jan once he's got her safely? Because men do change once they've got a woman and don't have to fight for her. Or so I've heard. And Jan would be terribly hurt——"

She broke off, because Nicolas had given a sudden exclamation which seemed almost to be one of pain. She turned in surprise to look at him. His brows were drawn and his face seemed lined with hurt.

"If he was cruel to Jan——" he began, and then stopped short and caught hold of Sarah-Ann's wrist. The grasp hurt her but she knew he did not even realize this. She had never seen him like this before. She longed to comfort him, though what she had to comfort him about she had no idea. But she was at a loss for words. If only she had had a little more experience! She felt young and useless and rather afraid.

He went on, "A time comes when you've got to unburden yourself to someone. I expect later I shall feel ashamed of bothering you with my troubles. You're such a child, and children should have gay, happy lives and not be pulled into unhappiness. But we've been such good friends and you've grown up so much lately."

She stared at him with her eyes widening and her soft lips trembling a little. Because his emotion half frightened her; because he had spoken of her as though she were still a little girl. Like the eldest White girl or any of the other schoolchildren on the island. Her heart began to sink. Something terrible was going to happen; she was sure of it. She tried to set her lips; she tried to look understanding and merely friendly, but she thought her heart had stopped beating and she wished it would do so really and never start again.

Because he was saying, in that hoarse voice as though the words were being drawn out of him because they must come although he did not want to admit them, "You see, I love Jan. More than anything in the world. I was such a fool that I only realized it when Luis had wormed himself in and made her love him. So I've no hope. But I can't stand by and see her made unhappy. I've got to do something to make sure he won't hurt her."

CHAPTER EIGHTEEN

A SHAFT OF sunlight pushed its way through the tree overhead. It fell, dappled black and gold, on the bonnet of the car. Sarah-Ann found herself watching it with fixed intensity.

She was two people. One was sitting, straight and rather prim, hands folded in her lap, eyes fixed steadfastly on Nicolas. The other was a quivering mass, mortally wounded, heart aching with a pain she had never known it could feel, her whole body an agonizing protest.

She must not let Nicolas know. That was her first wild, unreasoning thought. He must not realize that, while he was looking upon her as a child, imagining he was treating her like a kid sister, she was storing up every word of his, every smile, every shared thought, thinking that this was love. This gradual drawing together, this unfolding of hopes and longings. But she ought to have known. She ought to have told herself that love did not come that way. Or not always. Sometimes, perhaps, it grew slowly from liking and friendship. But more often, she tried to assure herself, it was like that shaft of sunlight, bursting suddenly upon the beauty of the world beneath.

She pressed her lips tightly together. She had grown up and that was the tragedy of it. A month or two ago she would have thrown herself upon him, raging and storming, telling him that no one but herself should ever have him. And then she would have cried, and some of the bitterness and anguish would have been washed out of her with her tears and she would have gone back home to be comforted by her old nannie.

But now no one could comfort her and she had to pretend. She had to remember as hard as she could that she must have pride, that she must hide away the wound she had received and go on just as if nothing had happened

She managed to twist her lips into a smile of reassurance. Her throat felt as though it were strangling her, but she managed to speak words that sounded slightly hoarse but otherwise just as they usually did. She said, "We won't let her be unhappy, Nick. We'll find some way."

He smiled, then. A twisted smile that did not look amused and yet was very gentle.

"You dear child!" he told her. "You're very sweet. But things aren't as easy as all that, I'm afraid. We can't go to Jan and say we're sorry but we don't think Luis would make her happy, so she'd better break it off and marry me instead."

Sarah-Ann stiffened. After all, Jan loved Luis, incredibly bad taste though it might seem, and not Nick. Perhaps there was some chance. You heard about hearts being caught on the rebound. But, right inside her, she knew that she was only thinking this because she did not want to give up hope. But it might happen. She clung tightly to this idea to stop herself from showing the tearing pain of her heart.

He went on, "I told myself at first, when I saw them growing more and more friendly, that I'd no right to interfere. I'm not well off and never likely to be. He's a millionaire and a very well-known one. What could I give her in comparison with that? Besides, although he has had so many girl friends, he has never even pretended to be serious with any of them. Jan has been different from the start and I thought that perhaps he would be faithful always to her. I knew he was unscrupulous, but Jan seemed to have softened him. Perhaps she has; perhaps I'm getting all worked up about nothing. It's just that it looks as though he hasn't given up his underhand tricks to try to get hold of Golden Grove, and if he can still do that, he can still do all the other things that would break Jan's heart."

"If he hadn't." Sarah-Ann's voice was nothing but a breath. "If he really loved her and if he didn't want to swindle other people because he knew what she would feel about it, what would you do then?"

He shrugged his shoulders.

"What could I do? If I felt reasonably sure she would be happy, I should wish her joy and just fade into the background. When you really love, little Sarie-Ann, you want the happiness of the person you love more than anything else. You'll learn that one day."

She put her hand up to her heart because it felt as though it were breaking right in half. But he had shown her now what she ought to do. Because if she really loved him, she would want him to be happy, so she would have to try to get Jan for him. She wanted to hate Jan but she couldn't. She was horribly jealous, but it wasn't the sort of jealousy she used to feel. When she would hit back as hard as she could and try to make the other person miserable. Now it was just a longing that filled her till there seemed no room for anything else.

"What will you do?" she asked at last.

"Try to find out what's going on," he answered. "We may be all wrong. Anyway, cheer up, infant. You look as if you'd lost your favourite toy. I'd no right to burden you with my troubles, you poor scrap! They just seemed too much for me, but I'm a fine one—pouring them out into your ears!"

She forced a smile. So that had been his idea of her all the time—a child who still liked the play with toys! That, she thought, was the unkindest cut of all!

She managed to say, "I'm glad you told me. I'm honored. And I won't tell a soul. I promise."

But then things were too much for her. She couldn't stay with him any longer; she couldn't talk to him as though only he were sad. She jumped up in such a hurry that she hit her head against the top of the car, but without stopping to answer his, "Have you hurt yourself?" she tugged open the door and jumped out.

"I'd better see Garth again," she murmured, and fled before he could stop her. She heard him call out, "Hi! Wait! I'll run you home." But she did not want that to happen. She wanted to be alone.

She rushed towards the cliff. No one was there now. It was the siesta hour, when all work on the fields and in the houses stopped and everyone slept. She had to be alone. Like animals when they were in pain and hurt. She couldn't bear to hear anyone, see anyone, speak to anyone. There was a belt of trees, not very far from the point at which Nicolas had put her down, and she made for that, blindly, unthinkingly.

Once she reached it she threw herself down, unmindful of snakes or any of the insects that abounded in the woods. She crumpled up till she lay full length, her face buried in the undergrowth.

It was only an hour ago that she had said proudly to herself, "When Nicolas and I are married," and now he didn't love her; he never had loved her; worst of all, he didn't think of her as someone old enough to be loved like that at all. At first she thought she would show him how wrong he was. Perhaps if she let him see how grown-up she was, if she made herself look particularly attractive and pretty—in a sophisticated and adult sort of way, of course—then he would turn to her for comfort and from comfort to love.

But then she wouldn't be herself. And she couldn't really carry it off; she knew she couldn't. She wished she could scream and cry and make him notice her. But those days were long gone by. She just had to stand in the background. And she couldn't stand it—she couldn't! She would probably fade away and die like girls in the olden days. But they never seemed to do that now; they just went on, getting more brittle and hard, because that was the only way of hiding their feelings, until, perhaps, they had no feelings left to hid. And she didn't want to be like that. She supposed she would be a dried-up old maid; certainly she would never marry. And she wouldn't be able to start the day nurseries she was thinking about because she couldn't bear to see Nicolas every day.

This last memory was too much for her. She burst into great racking sobs and lay there, choking and crying quite uncontrollably.

Suddenly she felt an arm round her. She was pulled up, and a large and not quite clean handkerchief wiped away her tears.

"What a sight you look!" Garth said, pulling her into his arms. "Crying doesn't suit you."

"You're a beast!" she began. "I don't want to talk to you!" But then her misery became too much for her and she wailed, "Oh, Garth, I'm so unhappy!" while fresh tears rolled down her cheeks.

"So I see." His tone was dry, but his arms held her closely to him and they were strong and gentle and comforting. She laid her head on his shoulder without really realizing what she was doing.

"Nicolas doesn't love me," she choked over the words. "I thought he did."

He grinned down at the top of her head, but his voice was gentle as he said, "And your heart's broken? Never mind, poppet; hearts don't really break."

"Well, why do they hurt so much?" she wanted to know.

"It hurts like hell after you've had an operation," he reminded her. "But after a time the wounds heal and never give you any more trouble. How old are you, sweet? Seventeen?"

"Eighteen," she answered with dignity, adding truthfully, "Just. But quite old enough to know my own mind."

His eyes smiled down at her.

"If I may be allowed to make a prophecy, I should say your heart will be broken another half-dozen times before it settles down to true love," he told her. "I can't quite remember how many times I decided I was going to die from love, and yet here I am, whole in body and mind."

"But you're different." It struck her suddenly that her old habit of considering everyone else's feelings as much less acute than hers was, perhaps, not such a good one after all. She peered up into Garth's pleasant, plain face and tried to think of him as having been as much in love with some girls as she was with Nicolas. It seemed impossible, so she finished rather weakly, "You weren't in love with Nick."

He threw back his head and roared with laughter.

"Heaven forbid!" he exclaimed. "But seriously, infant, you'll get over this. Some day. You'll find someone else." He paused for a moment and then went on bravely, because he was longing to tell her that she need not move from the spot to find someone who loved her with all his heart, but was afraid of frightening her away, "You'll leave the island and you'll find a dozen men in love with you and you'll love one of them back again. Perhaps several."

At the moment she did not believe that she could even look at any other man, but she decided that it was useless to tell him so. She realized, too, that she had been unburdening herself to him, crying on his shoulder and treating him to a quite deplorable lack of pride on her part.

She could not even imagine how she had come to tell him everything. He had caught her at a disadvantage, and to show that the subject was closed and she did not intend it to be reopened, she drew away from him, rubbing her hands across her face to try to eradicate the marks of tears. She knew she must be looking perfectly terrible, eyes red and swollen and cheeks puffy, but the trouble was, she couldn't find her own handkerchief.

She searched desperately for it in the pockets of her shorts, while Garth stood by looking at her critically. At last he said. "You've only made it worse, you know. You've smeared dust all over your face now. Why not borrow my handkerchief? Here you are. Spit, as Nannie always used to say to us when we were children. A simple if primitive way of making your face clean."

Whereupon, he carefully wiped the dust off her upturned face and then bent to implant a soft butterfly of a kiss on her parted lips.

"Garth Owen, I am not a child!" she reminded him crossly as she pulled herself away. "And I won't be treated like one! You'd better go now. What were you doing here, anyway?"

"Crumbs! If I hadn't forgotten!" he exclaimed. "I wanted to warn Nicolas and I was told he'd gone this way in his car. I was walking along hoping to catch up with him when I heard you boo-hooing and came to see what was wrong."

"I wasn't boo-hooing; I was being most restrained," she began hotly, but broke off to ask. "Why did you want to warn Nick? Is anything wrong?"

"Yes. Trouble with a capital T," Garth replied. "It seems that old Nick threatened to turn the Westons out and take their children away from them. Isaac went to Ben Grant with a tale of woe and he got hold of all the other trouble-makers on the island. They're drinking hard now and working themselves up into a sufficient state of courage to attack him. They say they're going to burn down Golden Grove. This rabble is in the minority, of course, but they're armed and the decent island people aren't. There's going to be trouble, I'm afraid, and Nick ought to be warned at once."

CHAPTER NINETEEN

JAN CAME DOWN the hill after her visit to Moses Lawson feeling much more composed and settled in her mind than she had done for a long time. The old man's simple philosophy and faith were touching. When she was with him, all the complications and worries seemed to iron themselves out, and she left, still with the glow of his simplicity upon her. There was nothing wrong that could not be put right. The fault until now, she decided, had been her own uncertainty. Roderick's image had grown gradually dim. Well, that was how it ought to be in this world. Nicolas had been right; she had been in love with Roderick, with his charm and good looks and forcefulness, but he had not been the one love. Her fault had been in her uncertainty since then. She had given in to Luis' plausibility, trying to persuade herself that she was in love with him. She wasn't; she had enjoyed his company, been thrilled by his practised love-making and, perhaps, rather flattered that he, who had so many women in love with him, should want to marry only her. That was not love, but she would have to make it do. She had promised to marry him, and she could not be unfair to him by backing out now. He had done nothing wrong.

She was able, now, to think of her scene with him that morning with pity and sympathy. If he sensed her lack of true love—as he must have done—it was no wonder that he was jealous and uncertain of her. Well, she would give him no cause for that in future. She would make herself love him and stop thinking so much about the hospital. She started to run down the hill, longing to meet him and tell him so.

She saw the hospital in the distance, gleaming in the sunlight. She saw the belt of trees between it and Golden Grove and—— She stopped short, her breath catching, staring down on the scene with a heart that was pounding with sudden fear.

What was happening down there? A crowd had gathered round the gates of the house. A threatening crowd. She could guess that from their gestures; flourishing of sticks and machetes, shouts which came to her faintly in the distance. Someone picked up a stone and threw it, breaking one of the windows.

The door opened and Nicolas came out. She saw him standing there, could make out that he was talking to the men. But they wouldn't let him; they were shrieking him down.

Jan had not known that she could run so quickly. Slipping on loose stones, sliding, slithering. What did a few bruises and scratches matter? She had to reach Nicolas! They were going to hurt him and they must not! She did not know what had happened and just now it did not matter. She had heard of mob madness, one man sweeping all the others on like sheep. This was happening now.

She passed a small group of island men and women, standing hesitantly outside their cottages, their faces frightened and glum.

"What are you doing?" She paused for a moment to shout out at them. "Are you a lot of mice to stand by and see these men from the other islands attack Golden Grove and Dr. Nick? Your Doctor Nick. Why don't you do something?"

The men shuffled their feet. One of them said in a shamefaced manner. "They're armed, Missy. They got guns and knives. We got nothing."

"Well, doesn't loyalty to the Duncarrons, who are part of you, matter more than that?" she asked, as another put in, "They be drinking, Missy. They roaring wild. They'll kill. You stay here with us."

"I won't! I'm going to help. I don't care if they've got a hundred guns and are all fighting drunk!" she cried. "And if any of you had got the courage of sheep, you would come along too."

She saw them shuffling, hesitating. She knew they were torn between loyalty and liking for the Duncarrons and fear. Fear of the blood-lust of a mob. But she had no time to be afraid herself. Only Nicolas mattered, standing there, facing the hostile crowd alone.

As she reached the outskirts of the group, Ben Grant put out a hand to stop her. He was dead-cold sober, she saw, using his wits to incite the others.

"You go back home, Nurse," he advised her. "We've got no quarrel with you. It's them from Golden Grove who are going to pay."

"Pay for what?" she asked, her voice clear and contemptuous, rising above the screams and shouts of the mob. "For being kind to you? For giving you medical attention and care? For letting you have a hundred and one things that aren't in your wages, and making this the best-run estate for hundreds of miles around? Is that what you're going to pay them for? With stones and guns and knives?"

"He's putting Isaac Weston out of his hut. He's taking his children away from him. He's a power-mad dictator. That's all he is. Grinding the faces of his workers in the mud while he lords it here with servants to wait on him and men sweating in the sun." Ben Grant's eyes slid shiftily away from hers, but his voice rose, overpowering her scornful tones which had made one or two of the men turn to look at her.

It wasn't any use, she knew. They wouldn't even listen. She could not get through the tightly packed masses to reach Nicolas, and, with sudden blinding clarity, she knew that if they killed him, she would want to kill them, too. She would not want to live. Without him, the hospital, her work she had found so engrossing would be nothing at all. Nicolas was the only person who mattered

She heard a howl like that of mad dogs. She saw someone raise a hand. She saw, above the head of a man who had moved, a stone hurtle through the air to catch Nicolas on the temple. He went down and the mob surged forward. If they threw themselves upon him, in their present madness—— She shuddered. She dared not think of the unthinkable, but she was wedged in here, unable to move, unable to make herself heard, and there was nothing she could do.

A strong arm caught hold of her and pulled her backwards so sharply that she was dragged to the edge of the crowd.

"Don't want you getting yore pretty frock wet, Missy,"

she heard Bill White's voice say. "But them niggers—they want their heads cooling and that's what they're going to get."

She turned, stumbling. The huge negro was standing by her, one of the great hosepipes that watered the land during the dry season in his hands. Before she could speak, before she could properly realize what he intended to do, he had turned it full on the mob. Water spouted out in a great deluge, soaking the mob, choking them with the streams that ran down their open mouths, getting in their eyes so that they could not see, pouring down their clothes.

Jan's legs were weak. She held on to a tree behind her. She saw, through eyes that were misted now with heat and shock, that others of the islanders had hosepipes on the other side of the crowd. Wherever the men turned, they were met with blinding deluges of water. Attacks with fists, with guns, with machetes, they could have put up with and, drink-maddened as so many were, have returned with interest. But this constant stream of water, throwing them into soberness and the realization of what they had been doing, was too much for them. They turned to run away, but Bill and his friends were there, an all sides of them, hosepipes levelled at them.

"We'll shut them up in the hospital to cool them a bit more." Bill grinned at her as he rounded the attackers up and marched them off. "Bella's gone; went when she heard what was up, so it'll make a fine lock-up for them."

He was thoroughly enjoying himself, but Jan had no time to listen to him. The hospital might be needed. For Nicolas. What had happened to him when that stone had struck him? She pushed through the now thoroughly demoralized mob and rushed towards the verandah.

He was lying there still, unconscious. She forgot she was a nurse; she forgot all about first aid and helping wounded men. She only knew that he was the man she loved and that he was lying unconscious. He couldn't be dead? Not Nicolas!

She knelt by his side, feeling his pulse. It was still beating, weakly and erratically. She thought he had concussion. She hoped his injuries were no worse, but how could she tell, out here, with nothing to help her? She felt his head carefully, lifting it on to her lap. Her eyes were so full of tears that she could not even see him properly. And then she heard the sound of running feet, and looked up to see Sarah-Ann coming chasing towards them.

Sarah-Ann! She was the one who ought to be by Nicolas' side. The present returned to Jan; she was no longer alone with Nicolas and her newly recognized love; Sarah-Ann was the girl he would want to see when he first recovered consciousness. Jan pulled herself together and rose to her feet.

"I don't think he's very seriously injured," she said, without knowing in the least whether he were or not. "Come here by him, Sarah-Ann. I'll go and fetch water to bathe his head and try to find out how badly hurt he is."

Sarah-Ann took a step forward, coloring a little; then she moved back.

"No, you stay there; it's your place," she said with a small break in her voice. "I'll go and fetch the water."

"You're the nurse, Jan," Garth reminded her, as he came up the verandah steps towards them. "Go ahead. Sarah-Ann and I arrived rather late on the scene, anyway."

Yes, she was the nurse. She was forgetting that. She was thinking of Nicolas only as the man who she knew now meant all the world to her. The one love she had found too late. She pushed thought away as she turned back to him.

"We ought to move him to his bed, oughtn't we?" Garth was asking. "But I daren't try to do it alone. Where are Leslie and Griselda?"

No one had thought of them before. Surely Leslie wouldn't leave Nicolas alone to take the brunt of the mob's fury? Jan and Garth stared blankly at each other, till Sarah-Ann emerged from the house pushing Griselda in front of her.

"I found her hiding in her bedroom having hysterics," she said coldly. "I told her she'd better come and help with Nicolas and make herself useful for once in her life."

Griselda was flushed from the scorn with which Sarah-Ann had scourged her. It was treatment to which she was not used, but she was uncomfortably aware that it was merited. She said weakly, "You know my nerves won't stand it. And if Leslie had been here I'd have stood by him, but he went out to see Mr. Anderson and I don't know what's happened to him."

"He's probably talking to Dad without an idea of what's been happening," Sarah-Ann told her, without troubling to keep her feelings out of her voice. "He'll be all right there; those rotters confined their attention to Golden Grove. Are you going to help us or not?"

She must, Griselda decided, pull herself together and show them that they were not the only heroines. She was feeling rotten, but she could not bear to be considered less resourceful than the others. If people were going to be thanked for their share in putting things to rights after the riot, then she was going to be one of the foremost of them. So she bustled out to the kitchen to encourage the maids and see that water was put on to boil.

Jan, meanwhile, had managed to become purely professional in her manner. Thank goodness, she thought, as she examined Nicolas' head, there did not seem to be any harm except concussion caused by his fall. If the stone had gone just a fraction of an inch nearer his eye—— She shuddered and then made herself face the fact that she must never think of what might have been. Only what was.

Bill White came tramping across the ruined garden amongst the torn flowers and shrubs, and across the pools of water still running over the muddied lawn. His broad face was one huge grin of satisfaction, and when Jan remembered how he had averted an extremely nasty situation in which there would probably have been murder, her heart went out to him.

"Bill, you were wonderful!" she cried, and in her relief she threw her arms round his neck and hugged him. "Whatever gave you such a brilliant idea?"

He grinned happily.

"Thank you, Missy," he said. "That the best way I've been greeted for years! Why, Missy, I knew them gasbags were nothing but roar and thunder, afraid of good clean water. I knew how to sober 'em up. And mighty ashamed of themselves they'll be when they come to properly! All except that Ben Grant, and he'll find no one'll listen to him again now. They've learnt their lesson. Grinding the faces of the poor workers, indeed! He'll be lucky, Missy, if he doesn't find his own face ground pretty hard!"

Then he saw Nicolas still lying on the verandah and exclaimed, "Dr. Nick—he ain't dead?"

At the horror in his voice, Jan warmed to him still further.

"He'll get better," she said, but she had scarcely finished speaking when he cut in with, "This ain't no place for him. I'm ashamed of you leaving him lying here!" Whereupon, he picked Nicolas up in his arms as easily as if he had been a child, in spite of his height and size, and carried him into the house.

Jan went with him to show him the room. As Bill put him gently down on the bed, he turned to Jan and said solemnly. "Don't forget, Missy, that if it hadn't been for him —and for you—I'd be dead now. And you were both that kind to my poor missus that she wasn't afraid when she drifted away from us all. I guess I owe you both more than I can ever repay, and I didn't do half as much as I might have done today. As I'd like to have done. I didn't stop this——"

"But he'll be all right!" Jan's voice rose a little; it was so unthinkable that he should be anything else. Nicolas would be all right; of course he would be!

When she had bathed and bandaged his head and done all she could for him, she sat awhile by his bedside. Leslie had come home; she could hear him in the garden trying to put back some order into its trampled ruins. The workers who had helped Bill were there too; those who had been too afraid to join in were running around being most vociferous as if to show their loyalty, even if it was at a rather late stage. Time had passed. Jan did not know how long, but glancing out of the window she saw that the sun had moved to the west and evening was approaching.

She sat there, battling with herself. A little while ago things had seemed so simple. She was going to fall in love with Luis; she was going to make him a good wife. And now, everything had changed. And yet nothing had. She was still engaged to Luis; he was still in love with her and she still owed him all the gratitude she had done before. She remembered his words—he would never let her go; she was the only woman in the world for him. Could she let him down now?

And Nicolas was still in love with Sarah-Ann. Jan could never marry him. But could she marry Luis? What ought she to do?

As her thoughts whirled round in circles, Nicolas opened his eyes. He looked at her and put out one hand in a blind, uncertain way.

"Darling!" he said, stumbling over the words. "I don't remember what has happened, but it's worth anything to have you here with me. Stay with me, darling."

"Yes, I'll stay," she said. For one moment, her heart had leapt with a joy that was almost more than she could bear, and then it sank again. He thought she was Sarah-Ann. Well, she would pretend to be until he was well enough to recognize faces. And then—she was still engaged to Luis; she had never yet in her life broken a promise and she was not going to start now. Neither Luis nor Nicolas should ever know the truth of her feelings for them.

CHAPTER TWENTY

NICOLAS' SLEEP NOW was a natural one. Jan was filled with relief. She wished she could have had an X-ray taken to make sure, but she did not think that his sleep would have been so calm and peaceful if there had been any other injuries. After a time someone called her and she went out to see what was wanted.

Things seemed to be more or less back to normal now. The estate workers had helped in force to clear up the trampled, soaked garden, all vying to show their loyalty. Inside the house the maids, who had been hiding trembling in the kitchen, had emerged to cook a meal and tidy the room whose window had been broken. The whole episode might never have been. And yet it had so nearly been tragedy. Jan thought of the men shut up in the hospital and wondered how they were faring.

"I'm letting them go after a good lecture," Leslie said in answer to her question. "There'll have to be an inquiry, but they're likely to have so uncomfortable a time with the islanders that they'll wish they'd never even thought of coming here. A lot depends on Nicolas. He will be all right, won't he, Jan? It seems unthinkable without him; it's only now I realize how much we've all depended upon him. Myself most of all."

She answered the appeal in his voice.

"I think he will," she replied. "I really believe it. He's sleeping so naturally now that I don't think there can be any great hurt done."

"Sleeping, is he?" Leslie's face cleared. "Well, then, I wonder whether you could go and look in on Griselda. I didn't like to ask you when I thought you were needed to stay with Nicolas, but if he's asleep, I wish you would. I've persuaded her to go to bed. This was such a terrible shock to her that she's all to pieces now, poor child. I don't know how she stood it—I shall never cease to blame myself because I wasn't here to look after her."

"There's no need to do that." Jan could not keep the dry note of coldness out of her voice, although she knew it would only annoy Leslie without having any other effect. "She seemed to manage quite well."

"Yes." In his eagerness, he had failed to note the sarcasm she could not hide. "She was absolutely marvellous, I know. She has told me how she helped you all, and how she was preparing to face the men alone when Bill White brought out the hosepipes. She's ready to face up to things when she has to; there's an unbreakable streak of courage in her. But you know how fine-drawn she is; when it's all over she feels it all the more, and that's the time she's inclined to go to pieces. So I do wish you'd see how she is and give her a sedative if she needs it."

Jan compressed her lips. Griselda had obviously got in her account of her doings; Jan wondered exactly what deeds of heroism she was supposed to have done. But it was pointless—it would even be cruel—to give Leslie the true version. So she contented herself with saying. "I'll look in on her in a minute or two."

Sarah-Ann and Garth were coming in from the garden together. Sarah-Ann's face was pale; there were dark smudges under her eyes and a look of utter strain and weariness that sagged her shoulders and drooped her mouth. Jan felt conscious-stricken. Sarah-Ann had worked so hard and she must be nearly driven wild with worry about Nicolas.

So, instead of going straight to Griselda, she stopped to say to Sarah-Ann, "Sit down and rest for a minute. Or would you like to sit with Nicolas? He's asleep now and it looks as though he'll wake up really better. You'll stay the night here, won't you? You look done in and we can let your father know."

Sarah-Ann's lips twisted into a smile that seemed as forced as her overbright voice when she spoke

"No, thanks. I really think I ought to go home. You know what Dad's like—he worries so terribly. I'm most awfully glad Nick is going to get better quickly, but I couldn't do him any good. Not like you. So I think it would be better for me to go home."

Jan's eyes were puzzled. This was not in the least like

Sarah-Ann. If this had happened yesterday, she would have refused to leave Nicolas' side. And though, of course, she was not a trained nurse, she had picked up enough in her work at the hospital to be able to be quite a lot of use in a sickroom. However, perhaps she felt too tired; she certainly looked it, so Jan made no remark.

"Don't bother about Sairey-Ann, Jan, I'm taking her home. I'm looking after her now," Garth said and put his arm round Sarah-Ann's bowed shoulders.

There was a possessive air about him that made Jan look at him in surprise. And Sarah-Ann did not seem to resent it as she would have done a few days ago. She smiled somewhat wanly at him, and then, saying to Jan, "I'll ring up from home to find out how Nick's getting along," she turned away, leaning on Garth slightly more heavily than was absolutely necessary.

Jan watched them go. She heard Sarah-Ann's voice as she said, "You're terribly good to me, Garth. I didn't know you could be so nice," and his rejoinder, "Being good to you isn't difficult, my precious; I like it. The more the better."

Surely, thought Jan, her brows meeting in a frown of anxiety, surely Sarah-Ann wasn't going to let down Nicolas just when he most needed her? She was very young, of course; young for her age, even, for she was so untried. But she had loved Nicolas so intensely. It would be cruel if she threw him over for Garth just at this time of all others.

She sighed and then, remembering Griselda, hurried along to her room.

Griselda was sitting up in bed, looking pale and interesting. The pale-blue pillows behind her head matched the soft blue bedjacket she was wearing and the ribbon tying back her wonderful red-gold hair. She closed her eyes when Jan entered the room, a saintly martyred look stealing across her features

"I can't stand this life any more, Jan," she murmured weakly. "It'll kill me. You know it's too much for me—you know I can't stand things the way you can."

Jan sat down with a plomp on the end of the bed. "Open your eyes and look at me when you talk to me," she rapped out. When there were so many people really needing care and attention, Griselda's affectations were too much for her.

Griselda's eyes shot open in surprise and she looked at Jan warily and defensively.

"You're cruel, Jan——" she was beginning, when Jan cut into her words.

"No, I'm not; I'm talking sense," she replied abruptly. "It would have been a great deal better for you if we'd all done that before, instead of letting you think you could get away with tantrums and spite and lies and behaving as if you needed wrapping up in cotton-wool and treated with the utmost delicacy. There's nothing wrong with you that you can't control yourself. You behaved like a coward this afternoon and you know it. But, because you won't face up to facts, because you always have to be in the limelight, you persuaded yourself that you're ill and that's why you couldn't stand up to danger. You had to lie to Leslie to try to make yourself out a heroine, so that he would fuss over you and make you feel you really are all you pretended to be. But you can't go on forever making other people miserable and forcing yourself to the front whether you deserve the place or not. You've got to pull yourself together while you're able to, or a time will come when you find you can't."

Griselda's glance was sidelong. Her lips quivered and she burst into tears. But they were quiet tears, not hysterical sobs, and they almost made Jan feel ashamed of herself. But she must not allow herself to be sidetracked. For Griselda's own sake. So she waited silently, till Griselda pulled a tiny lace handkerchief from beneath her pillow and tried to mop her eyes on its inadequate square.

"I'm sorry, Jan," she said, between sobs. "I wanted to be angry, but I can't because it's true. You needn't think I don't know it. I do; after I've said something horrible or pushed myself into the limelight, as you call it, I feel absolutely ghastly. I lie awake at night often, feeling ashamed and making up my mind I won't do it again, but I do. I just can't help it."

"But, Griselda——" Jan was beginning when Griselda went on, "The trouble is, this isn't my sort of life and I'm far too weak a character to stand up to it. I'm a different sort of person when I'm at home. I've got my own friends —people I've got things in comomn with—and I feel myself being nice and good-tempered and charitable. But as soon as I get out here—oh, Jan, do persuade Leslie to go home. He got the offer of a job at home a month or so ago. He refused it, but it may still be open, and, if not, he'd soon get another with his experience."

"But he would hate it," Jan protested. "He loves Golden Grove and he would loathe any other sort of job."

Griselda shook her head.

"No, you're wrong," she answered. "It's Nick who adores Golden Grove. Leslie would leave it quite happily, but he feels it would be letting Nicolas down. And the job is manager of a big farm in England, so it would be the same sort of work. And though I'd be in the country, I would be within reach of town and my friends."

"You see," she went on, as Jan was silent, trying to sort this all out, "he talked to me when the offer came. It was through a friend of mine, as a matter of fact. Leslie was tremendously keen on the idea at first; he says the responsibility of running an estate here on a shoestring is too much, and he thinks if we settled at home we might be able to start a family. He longs for that. I do too, secretly, but I pretend I don't want kids because I don't seem able to achieve it. Anyway, at first he was keen. And then he heard Nick talk about hating the very idea of selling Golden Grove and loving every inch of it, so Les never told him about the offer. He said he couldn't leave him to work it all alone. But I've been thinking and it might be a good thing for Nick. You know how keen he seems on Sarah-Ann—though I can't think what he sees in her—but it might be difficult for him to bring a wife home to a household like this. Young couples need to start on their own. I know, because I've never had a chance to be alone with Les."

All this was so completely new to Jan that she needed time to think it over. Her voice was comforting and sympathetic as she said, "I must think about it. I hadn't known any of that, you see. But you must go to sleep now and not worry any more. I'll give you something to help you to sleep."

"Thank you." Griselda sounded like a polite child now.

She leaned forward to say, "You'll move over from the hospital tonight and sleep here, won't you?"

Jan shuddered. The idea of sleeping in the hospital where the rioters had been imprisoned was a horrible one. Besides, Nicolas might need her. So she answered soothingly, "Yes; I'll be here. You'll only need to call if you want me."

Griselda lay back with a sigh of satisfaction, while Jan went to see what was happening at the hospital. Leslie, she found, had been across there, had frightened the men completely by telling them there would be an inquiry into the affair of the afternoon, but in the meanwhile they might go to their own houses. By now the hospital was empty. Lily had been across to tidy it up and remove all traces of the men's occupancy, and to all appearances it was just as it had been that morning. Only, to Jan, it would never feel quite the same.

Nevertheless, she had to collect her things from there if she was going to sleep at the house. So she walked across the quiet, dark way between the house and hospital. Her nerves were still slightly jangled, however, for she jumped when someone stepped out before her and stood in her way. When she saw that it was only Luis, her legs felt suddenly weak.

"Darling!" He put his arm round her. "You're trembling! I've been so worried. I didn't know anything about it till too late. You're not hurt, are you? You're sure you're not hurt?"

"I'm all right," she assured him. "Nicolas was the only casualty."

"How is he?" Luis asked quickly.

"He'll be all right, I think. Only"—she found herself shuddering again and could not stop—"it was awful, Luis. It would have been murder if it hadn't been for Bill White. They would have trampled him to death."

"Don't think about it!" Luis' arms were tightly round her. "It was bad. They should not have gone so far."

"They should not have gone any way at all!" Jan cried sharply. "What do you mean, Luis?"

"Nothing, my pet," he soothed her. "English is not my real language, you know. I think I am perfect in it and then I make a foolish mistake which makes my meaning all wrong. And I am worked up tonight. Worried about you. So I cannot think as well as I should. Jan, my sweet, this hasn't changed things, has it? You are still willing to marry me? Life would be quite barren for me without you."

Jan drew her breath in sharply. She thought of the hour she had sat by Nicolas' bed, thinking this very thing out. She remembered her resolution and she answered steadily, after only a moment's pause, "Why should it have changed anything? I—I'm afraid I don't love you as much as you love me, but if you're willing to put up with that, I'll marry you any time you want."

"Darling! I'm not afraid! I'll make you love me!" he cried, and would have drawn her into his arms, but at that moment they saw a dark form emerge from the trees and come towards them.

Jan shuddered.

"It's Ben Grant!" she cried. "He's a horrible man! An evil man! I don't want to see him!"

"And you needn't!" Luis kissed her lightly and then put her from him. "Run along to the hospital. I'll get rid of him and then come to take you back to the house. You ought not to be wandering about alone tonight."

"No one would hurt me," Jan protested, but, nevertheless, she went.

As she reached the hospital door, she heard Luis call out sharply, "That you, Grant? What are you doing here?" and then came Ben's reply, "I'm in trouble—real trouble now, Boss, and you've got to help me out. That's what."

CHAPTER TWENTY-ONE

JAN'S HAND WAS touching the hospital door; she kept it there, breath held, as she waited for some explanation of Ben Grant's extraordinary demand. Not that she had any intention of eavesdropping—but what could Luis have to do with the agitator? She felt it was her right to know.

But, before she could rejoin them, Luis took a quick step towards her.

"Leave me to settle this," he shot out in a tone of command. "It's nothing for you to worry about."

She shook her head.

"No, Luis," she answered. "I think I've a right to know what Ben meant. I am connected both with Golden Grove and with you. Why should he take it for granted that you should help him?"

"Because I've done it before." Luis ground the words out viciously. "And helped him by giving him a job which he bungled abominably in return. No, Grant; I've had enough; you can't expect any more help from me. I'll talk to you later—at my own convenience."

He took Jan's arm and started to steer her towards the house. She went, too puzzled to protest, walking slowly, almost blindly, in her bewilderment of mind.

"I don't understand——" she began questioningly.

"Listen, pet." Luis broke into her words, and though his voice was quiet there was an underlying note of impatience in it. "This is not my only business, you know. I have interests all over the world. In one of them, I met Grant and did my best to do him a good turn. Because of that, he seems—quite wrongly—to imagine he can call on me whenever he gets into a mess. That's all."

"But you never told me you knew him," she persisted. "When we mentioned him——"

He laughed, and stopped her words with a flicker of a kiss.

"You darling little idiot!" he said. "When I've had

thousands of men working for me, do you suppose I can remember them all? Grant brought himself to my notice, or I don't suppose I should have known who he was. But you're too tired to think straight. Run off to bed now and we'll talk about it tomorrow. Not another word—I insist! God bless, my sweet."

He gave her another light kiss and a gentle push towards the house; then he stood there waiting till she was inside and the door closed after her.

It was very quiet now. Everyone seemed to have decided that, after the excitements of the day, an early night was the only thing to be desired. Jan hadn't brought her things from the hospital, after all, she remembered. Never mind; she could manage without them. She didn't suppose she would get much sleep, anyway; she must keep an eye on Nicolas.

She peeped into his room, but he was still asleep, and at last she made up a bed for herself on a couch in the living-room, where she would hear any sound he made.

Her sleep was broken. Again and again she relived the horror of the moment when she was hemmed in in the midst of the maddened crowd, struggling to make them listen to words which would not carry above their angry roar, fighting to push through them to Nicolas. Again and again she saw Nicolas fall and felt the surge the mob gave as it pressed on to the kill. And then she would awake with a strangled cry, trembling with the vividness of it, till she slipped out of bed and tiptoed across the passage to make sure that Nicolas was still sleeping quietly.

The darkness, at last, was broken by shafts of grey. Dawn was coming and she was glad to get up, to sting energy back into herself with the sharp shock of an icy cold shower, to dress in clean uniform and brush her hair to sleekness before she pushed it under a cap and emerged, neat and well-groomed, hoping that this would hide her white face and heavy eyes.

The house was stirring now. She saw Leslie cross the yard towards the stables and, from the kitchens, an appetizing smell of coffee made her realize her hunger. She went out and took a cup from Lily, gulping it down quickly but feeling better after it.

"I'll make some for Dr. Nick," Lily told her. "He—he'll be well enough to drink it, won't he?"

"I hope so. I'm just going to see," Jan told her, and hurried back to Nicolas' room.

As soon as she opened the door, she saw his eyes, wide and clear, fixed upon her, and he gave her a warm smile.

"Hello, Jan," he said. "What on earth am I doing here like this? I've been trying to remember. A schemozzle with that wretched subversive element, wasn't it? Clear out of here now like a good child, will you? I'm going to get up and you shall tell me all about it while we have breakfast."

"You are most certainly not going to get up!" Jan faced him determinedly. "The very idea! You were knocked out and had concussion. Surely you as a doctor ought to know how foolhardly it would be to get up straight away. You'll stay in bed and I'll tell Lily to bring you your breakfast. Then we can talk about getting up."

"Bully!" He grinned at her teasingly. "You're in your element now, aren't you? Able to get back at me for all the difficult moments I've given you in the past. All right; I'll have my breakfast in bed, but only on the condition that you have it in here with me and tell me everything that happened."

That happened to be exactly what she wanted to do more than anything in the world, so she left him long enough to help Lily prepare an appetizing breakfast of coffee, toast and fruit. Lily's broad smile and thankful ejaculations when she brought in the tray made him look thoughtful.

"It seems as if everyone is thankful for my return to life," he said. "What happened, Jan? I remember haranguing the men and getting more and more livid because I couldn't make them listen to me and then—— What happened then?"

"Someone threw a stone." She told him of that and of Bill's brilliant inspiration in turning the hosepipes on the rioters till they were completely demoralized.

Nicolas threw back his head and roared with laughter.

"Bother—that hurts!" he exclaimed ruefully touching his head gingerly. "But it's so darned funny! Good old Bill! Who else would have thought of that?"

He grew serious then and added, "I expect he saved my life. They were after my blood, you know."

She shivered.

"I do know," she murmured.

He looked at her curiously.

"I have an idea," he remarked, "that when I was trying to gain their attention, I saw you right in the middle of them, doing rather better at making them listen than I was. Thank goodness you weren't hurt, my dear."

She flushed at the gentleness of his voice.

"Bill looked after me," she answered simply. And then, because she felt that this was a subject best steered clear of, she hurried to tell him everything else that had hapened.

"Nicolas," she said at last, "could you manage the estate by yourself if Leslie went home? To live, I mean."

He looked curiously at her.

"I guess so," he told her. "Lots of men do work an estate without a partner. But it's not likely to happen; Leslie loves the place as much as I do and he wouldn't leave here willingly."

"Has he told you so—in words, I mean?" Jan asked. "Or have you just taken it for granted because you love it so yourself?"

His brows were drawn as he moved a little to look more closely at her.

"What's all this about?" he asked. "What are you trying to tell me? Well, I don't know if Les has actually said in words, 'I love Golden Grove and I don't want to leave it.' He wouldn't, you know; one doesn't say things like that; one just feels them. But I always imagined he did; he certainly hasn't said the opposite. Why?"

"Because—I was talking to Griselda——" Jan burst into explanations. She was not sure whether she was betraying a confidence of Leslie's, but Griselda had not sounded as though she thought so.

At the end she looked at Nicolas. He was lying very still and she could not see the expression in his eyes. She was afraid, suddenly, that she had hurt him.

"Of course, Griselda might have made it up to serve her own ends," she finished on a lower note. "You know what she is."

Her voice trailed away beneath his unresponsiveness, but at this he turned quickly towards her.

"Yes, I know what Griselda is," he repeated. "It was she who wanted to go out in the yacht the day you were wrecked, wasn't it? You were the one who tried to persuade them not to go and, finally, you only went with them to look after her. I'm right, aren't I?"

She felt the color rush to her cheeks.

"How did you know?" she asked weakly. "Have you just guessed?""

"Oh, no," he replied. "I guessed a long time ago. At first I thought you really were to blame and I was furious with you, as I dare say you knew. But, bit by bit, I began to see how out of character it was. And how very much in Griselda's character. It was the way Luis backed her up that put me off at first. But I suppose he had his own reasons."

"Yes." Her heart was pounding painfully. Mention of Luis had brought everything back to her; her promise to him last night; the necessity for hiding her feelings from Nicolas. And when they were alone like this, when he was so friendly and affectionate, it was terribly difficult not to let him know how much every nice word he said meant to her.

So she pulled herself together firmly and said, "That has reminded me. Talking about Luis, I mean. I expect I shall be marrying him very soon. I don't want to leave you in the lurch and, of course, I shan't be able to work in the hospital after I'm married. So I thought I'd better prepare you so that you can start looking for another nurse straight away."

The animation left his face. His voice was hard and almost angry as he said, "Naturally the wife of the great Luis Corando can't be expected to work! I hope you realize that you're marrying a millionaire? But, of course, any girl would!"

She longed to keep the color from flooding her face, but she could not do so. She felt great waves of it burning her cheeks in angry humiliation. She was furious with him for a moment, and then very agonizingly ashamed of herself. Because anyone who even guessed the true state of affairs between her and Luis would imagine that his money had a great deal to do with it. It would be quite useless to expect them to believe anything else.

But before she could manage to bring out the words that struck in her throat, Nicolas put out his hand and caught hold of her.

"Jan! Don't look like that!" he exclaimed. "It was an absolute unforgivable thing for me to say! I didn't mean it —not a word of it! Can you ever forget it and just pretend it never happened at all?"

She nodded. She still found it impossible to speak, and he was looking at her with remorse and concern when a sound outside the open french windows made them both turn round to look at it.

Ben Grant was standing there, one hand on the latch, as he sidled his way inside.

Jan's breath caught in horror. She stared at his sullen, bad-tempered face, small eyes half hidden beneath bushy brows. She remembered with terrifying clearness the scenes of the day before. Ben's voice raised to encourage the mob and drive them on to murder. She found herself thinking desperately, he's come to finish off his work. Because Bill chased them off in time yesterday, he has come when there's no one about to kill Nicolas himself.

On the spur of this thought, she threw herself forward, shielding Nicolas from him.

"Go back!" she cried. "You're not to hurt him! I'll scream the place down if you come a step nearer!"

Nicolas pushed her gently aside. He kept his hand on hers, and the grasp was warm and reassuring. He looked at Ben Grant with cold, hard eyes, and there was a note of command in his voice as he spoke.

"All right, Jan; I'll manage this," he said, and then, to Ben, "Well, what is it, Grant? What do you want here?"

Ben's lips twitched in a grimace that was evidently intended to be a smile.

"Not to worry, Missy," he told Jan. "I wouldn't hurt Dr. Nick. Not now. I never had anything personal against him and I wouldn't have done it if I hadn't been paid to do so."

"Paid?' Nicolas' eyes narrowed. "So it is some labour

agitator at the bottom of it! But who on earth would bother about us here?'

Grant shook his head.

"Not that, sir," he said. "I have stirred up trouble of that sort before now, but I wouldn't have come here for that. And I wouldn't have told you this if him who engaged me wasn't trying now to slip out of it and leave me to take all the blame. Because I went too far, he said; because he hadn't wanted you hurt."

An agonizing fear had entered Jan's heart. She remembered suddenly the way Luis had greeted her news last night, the way Grant had accosted him, the lameness of Luis' explanations.

Her lips were dry as she asked, "Who paid you?" and when his answer came she felt as though she had known it all the time and yet could not bear to hear it.

"Why, Mr. Corando, of course," Ben Grant answered. "Luis Corando, who wanted to make you sell Golden Grove, sir, and turn you out of the island and away from Nurse Jan."

CHAPTER TWENTY-TWO

JAN, standing by Nicolas' side, knew quite clearly, she thought, what Ben Grant's further words would be, yet she could not bear to hear him say them. She was rigid as he went on to explain that Luis had met Grant in one of the other islands, that he had deliberately hired him to come to Dream Island with other picked men who could easily be stirred to discontent, that he had stooped to such deceit such violence, to what might so well have ended in tragedy, simply to gratify his desire for Golden Grove and his hatred of having his will crossed in any way.

She remained quite still, her hand in Nicolas'. She could not move. She felt as though she had been turned into a statue. Her heart was as heavy as lead with the shock and horror of it she could not even think.

Only when Nicolas had said, "That's all, Grant; you'd better go now. I don't know yet what's going to happen," and Ben had gone away, soft-footed as he had come, did she begin to feel some life seeping back into her as painfully as a foot may feel after it has "been to sleep."

"I'm sorry, Jan," Nicolas said gently.

The sympathy in his voice was too much for her. She slid down by the side of his bed, resting her head on the cover, and suddenly, without warning, she felt great choking sobs rising within her, racking her body with their pain.

"Oh, Nicolas, what am I to do?" she asked.

His hand hovered for a moment over her hair, touching it gently before he moved away. She could not see his eyes, nor the expression on his face as he looked down at her bent head.

"I feel so useless," he said. "I'd give anything in the world to help you, but I can't. No one can ever come near another's tragedy, however much they may long to take it away. And, knowing how you love Luis—— But perhaps your love will bring forgiveness with it."

She made a sudden movement, raising her face, regardless of the tears streaking it. Nicolas' words had stung her into self-reproach she could not let him go on thinking her fine and unselfish. There must be truth between them, whatever the future held.

"But I don't love him!" she cried. "That's the worst part of all! If I did, perhaps I would understand, perhaps I might influence him. But I was unfair to him in promising what I hadn't got to give him; I feel as much a traitor as he is. And I don't know what to do about it. I was lonely and sad and he was kind to me. I was fond of him; I thought perhaps it was love. A different sort of love. And then, suddenly, I found out the truth and I knew."

She broke off. She could not tell him any more, but she had forgotten that her eyes, raised in despair to his, spoke more plainly than her voice. He caught her face between his hands, looking down at her as though he could not quite believe what he saw there.

"Jan," he said slowly at last, "is it true? Didn't you know I've loved you for a long time now?'

And then, without giving her time to answer, he pulled her towards him and kissed her on her lips.

Jan's head was whirling and her heart seemed to be dancing backwards and forwards. She could not quite believe it; she could not think. She only knew that Nicolas had said he loved her and that he was kissing her as if it was something he had dreamed of for ages untold.

She did not know how long it was before they heard a cough from the direction of the french windows, and even then Nicolas only slowly let her go, still keeping hold of her hand.

Jan was glad of that. It gave her support, and that was what she needed now, for Luis was standing leaning against the post, watching them with an inscrutable face and a small, wry smile on his lips.

"I beg your pardon," he said. "It seems I intrude. I wished to inquire after you, Nicolas, and I could make no one hear at the front door, so I came round here. I must tell you that I regret what happened yesterday with all my heart."

"Even after instigating it?" Nicolas asked dryly.

Luis raised his eyesbrows.

"Ah, I see I have been found out," he said ruefully. "And that is the unforgivable sin—to be found out, is it not? I fear I am losing my grip. Love and business do not combine well, But may I be allowed to come in to state my case? In your English law a prisoner is always said to be innocent till found guilty, is it not?"

Without waiting for an answer, he walked into the room and, selecting a chair, sat down upon it to face them.

"I admit," he went on lightly, though his eyes were keen, "that in those old, gone days, before I met Jan, I hired Grant to stir up discontent here. I did not mean it to be any more than a certain amount of talk and unpleasantness, just to make you see that you might be wiser to sell the estate to me. Then I met Jan and you know what happened. I knew what she would think of such methods and decided to be done with them. I told Grant so. But then I had certain information which led me to become jealous of you, Nicolas. Not; it seems, without cause. So I decided that it would do you no harm to give you a fright. Those were my orders to Grant. But you played right into his hands by your treatment of Isaac Weston. Thoroughly deserved treatment, I may add. Grant jumped at this opportunity, but he went too far. I had no part in the attack on you; in fact, I had absolutely forbidden it. However, I must have lost my grip; I failed to take the human element into account. Worse still, I antagonized Grant by refusing to help him, since he had exceeded everything I told him to do. And he, I suppose, got his own back by telling the whole deplorable story."

There was a hint of mischief in his voice as he finished. He rose from his chair and came over to Jan.

"This is the place where I give you back your freedom," he told her. "I cannot expect you to marry me after this and I prefer to be the one to release you, rather than give you the trouble of breaking with me. It is, perhaps, as well. I am a bad lot, I think, and I probably always shall be. I would very likely break your heart, and since I truly love you, I should break my own in the process."

He took her hand in his. She tried to speak but she could not. She knew that he was selfish, unscrupulous and hard, but there was something about him that, as always, drew her sympathy and liking. And with it all, she believed that, when he said he really loved her, he did indeed mean every word.

He saw the mingled expressions on her face and laughed softly.

"Poor little Jan!" he said gently. "You are too soft-hearted—that is your trouble. I should very soon have crushed your heart, but Nicolas will take care of you. And they lived happily ever after, like the fairy stories. For you will work to make that come true; for it does need work, you know. And I will not have you grieve for me. When I am away from you, perhaps I will forget these few precious weeks I thoughtI had found the one and only girl. I shall find other girls—many of them—and I shall love each one just a little, and I shall thank my lucky stars that I did not let myself love too deeply with any."

Nicolas said abruptly, "Thank you, Luis. You've made up for everything, I think."

He shook his head, smiling.

"Not altogether, I think, but I will do," he promised. "For your wedding present, I will give you all the things for your hospital that I had promised to give if you sold Golden Grove. And, then, perhaps you will not altogether forget me, Jan? You will sometimes think of me and wonder how many girls I am flirting with and whether any of them will mean as much to me as you——"

He broke off, and for the first time he winced as though the pain were too much for him. But is passed almost at once. He said lightly, "Good-bye, my dear little Jan. I think perhaps I may be allowed a kiss, since it is the last I shall ever give you."

And, tipping up her face, he kissed her lips so lightly that she scarcely felt the touch.

"Good-bye, Luis," she said then, and realizing that it was the first time she had spoken since he had come into the room. "I'm—sorry."

He did not answer. He was smiling at them as he went out of the house, but Jan felt that her eyes were wet.

"I shall always like him," she said, and found that her voice was choked. "I shall aways feel sorry."

"But you will always love me," Nicolas broke gently into her words. "He was right, wasn't he, my sweet?"

She looked at him, forgetting Luis, remembering only the surprise and wonder of Nicolas' words and his kiss.

"But I thought you were in love with Sarah-Ann," she began.

"Sarah-Ann?" He laughed. "Why, she's only a child! She doesn't love anyone yet, though some day she will love with all her heart. She knows about my feelings for you. I told her yesterday."

Yesterday? So that explained Sarah-Ann's behaviour! Jan's admiration and liking went out to her. Little Sarah-Ann had, indeed, grown up to take it on the chin like that! Poor girl! But her secret would be safe with Jan. And, remembering Garth's proprietorial air the night before and the way Sarah-Ann had leaned upon him in her weariness of mind and body, Jan began to feel that, perhaps, soon, another romance would spring up there and that Sarah-Ann would be happy, after all.

But her mind was so full of her own love and happiness that she could not go on thinking of other people all the time. Luis and Sarah-Ann were both forgotten when Nicolas' arms were round her.

At last he said, "Now you've no excuse for treating me as an invalid any longer. Run along, my sweet, while I get dressed. Then we'll go and tell Leslie and Griselda that, if they really want to go home, they mustn't stop on my account because I shall have a wife here to look after me."

Jan left him and went to stand on the verandah, looking over the garden. It was almost impossible to think that yesterday it had been trampled into ruin. Many eager hands had repaired the scuffled turf of the lawn and replanted flowers which, with tropical exuberance, had sprung back to life. Nicolas came quietly behind her and put his arm round her. She rested her head on his shoulder and they stood there, without speaking, for a moment. Then Bill White came to the gate and stopped short, staring at them. He turned, then, to wave to someone behind him.

"They're here!" he cried. "Dr. Nick and Missy Jan. Our Missy Jan going to stay with us—with the Doctor!"

Jan smiled as the garden seemed to fill with cheering groups. Nicolas' arm was strong around her. She could look across the garden to the hospital in the distance. Her hospital—hers and Nicolas'. This was her life and these were her people. She moved forwards towards them, her hand in Nicolas', and knew that here, in these kindly surroundings, she had come to her journey's end.